STEP TO THE GRAVEYARD EASY

Also by Bill Pronzini

◆

BLUE LONESOME
A WASTELAND OF STRANGERS
NOTHING BUT THE NIGHT
IN AN EVIL TIME

STEP TO THE
GRAVEYARD EASY

Bill Pronzini

Walker & Company ❋ New York

First published in the United States of America in 2002 by
Walker Publishing Company, Inc.

Published simultaneously in Canada by Fitzhenry and Whiteside,
Markham, Ontario L3R 4T8

For information about permission to reproduce selections from this book,
write to Permissions, Walker & Company, 435 Hudson Street,
New York, New York 10014

Library of Congress Cataloging-in-Publication Data
Pronzini, Bill
Step to the graveyard easy / Bill Pronzini.
p.   cm.
ISBN 0-8027-3375-1 (alk. paper)
I. Title.
PS3566.R67 S73   2002
813'.54—dc21   2001055914

Series design by M. J. DiMassi

Printed in the United States of America

2 4 6 8 10 9 7 5 3 1

For Marcia

And the Spirit say, Go down, Death easy
I want you to go down, Death easy
I want you to go down, Death easy
And bring my servant home.

Step to the graveyard easy
I want you to step to the graveyard easy
I want you to step to the graveyard easy
And bring my servant home.
                              —"Go Down, Death"

STEP TO THE GRAVEYARD EASY

1

CAPE was screwing the little redhead from Logan's Café when Anna came home and caught him.

He didn't see or hear her walk into the bedroom. The redhead was on top, making pleasure noises, leaning forward with her breasts in his face. Neither of them knew Anna was there until she yelled, "You son of a bitch!" in a shrill tremolo.

The redhead wrenched around and off him so violently she damn near ruptured him. Anna was standing stick straight in the doorway. White face, white fisted hands, white nurse's outfit and cap. Like a ghost except for her eyes. They burned hot, smoky at the edges, like cigarette holes in a piece of paper before it bursts into flame.

None of them said anything. Anna stared at him; the redhead, Lonnie, stared at Anna; and he didn't look straight at either one. Lonnie was scrambling into her clothes, panting in a different cadence now. He heard her start to babble.

"Oh God, Mrs. Cape, I'm sorry . . . he said you wouldn't be home until late . . . I didn't mean to . . . I don't know why . . . oh God, I'm sorry . . ."

"Get out of here," Anna said. She didn't take her eyes off Cape.

"So sorry, really, I . . ."

"Get out of my house."

Lonnie ran out, holding her blouse closed with one hand, her bra trailing from the other. The front door slammed.

Anna said, "In our bed. Right here in our bed."

Cape swung painfully off the bed, stood up. He didn't say anything.

"You're such a shit."

"I guess I am."

"Put something on," she said, disgust in her voice. "She shines all over you like grease."

He bent, wincing, to pick up his pants. He put them on, put on his shirt. The doorway was empty by then. When he went out into the living room, Anna was at the sideboard pouring Scotch. The bottle's neck chattered against the rim of the tumbler. She'd pulled off her cap; her blond hair was frizzed up on top and sides like a fright wig. He moved past her to the front window, stood looking out.

Behind him she said, "Well?"

He didn't answer.

"No excuses? No apology?"

A kid went by on a bicycle, pumping hard, his long hair streaming out behind him.

"All right, then. Tell me this. Is she the first?"

Another kid, this one fat, working the pedals even harder and sweating in the muggy June heat. The type who would always be lagging behind, trying to catch up to the front-runners and never quite making it. The type Cape himself had always been.

"Answer me, Matthew."

No. Not really like that kid, not any longer. He'd quit pumping hard, trying to catch up; for some time now he'd just been standing still.

"Damn you, say something!"

"Would you believe me if I said Yes, she was the first?"

"No."

"Well, she was."

"Liar."

"Have it your way then."

"Why other women? Wasn't I enough for you?"

Cape turned to face her. Hurt and anger made her eyes as round and shiny as grapes. "You're woman enough for any man," he said.

"Then why? Why fuck somebody else in our bed?"

"I did it, that's all."

"You did it, but that's not all. Not by a long shot."

"The only answer I can give you is that I'm not the same."

"What does that mean? The same what?"

"Same man you married. I've changed. You haven't."

"Right, sure. That explains it."

"We've grown apart," Cape said. "Things haven't been good for either of us for some time. You know they haven't. We don't even have sex much anymore."

"Oh, so now you're going to use that as an excuse."

"I'm not making excuses."

"I can't help it if I've had so much night duty, long hours at the hospital."

"Not blaming you, Anna. Just stating a fact. The marriage isn't working."

"Maybe it isn't," she admitted, "but we could've worked things out. Twelve years . . . we made it through rougher patches . . ."

"In the beginning," Cape said. "We're different people now."

"You keep saying that. You're the one who's changed, that's for sure. The past few months . . . moody, restless . . . all that so-called business travel to Chicago or wherever . . . and now you bring another woman into our bed. I hardly know you anymore."

"No, not anymore."

"What's the matter with you? Some kind of midlife crisis, is that it? You're thirty-five, that's not even midlife."

"Three score and ten," he said.

"What?"

"Never mind. Forget it."

"Forget it," Anna said bitterly. "Am I supposed to forget what I just saw in the bedroom?"

"I don't expect you to, no."

"I couldn't if I wanted to. In *our* bed, damn you!" She swallowed Scotch, coughed, tried to drink again, and choked this time. She hurled the glass against the couch. "You bastard," she said. She was on the edge of tears now.

"I'm sorry, Anna. I know you don't believe it—"

"I wouldn't believe you anymore if you said the sky was blue."

"—but it's the truth. I'm sorry for everything."

"Liar. All you're sorry for is that you got caught."

"All right."

"All right, all right, all right." She drew a long, shuddery breath. "We're finished, Matthew. Once and for all, as of right now."

"I know."

"What you did today . . . it's the one thing I won't put up with."

"I know," he said again.

"You know, you know. You don't know *shit*, that's what you don't know."

"You're better off without me," he said.

"Well, that's for damn sure."

"I'll leave right now."

"The quicker the better. Pack up and get out. Go chase after that redheaded bitch, finish what you started."

"I'm through with her."

"You think I care? Screw her brains out, for all I care." Wetness dribbled along her cheek. Angrily she wiped it away. "One thing you better understand right now. I want this house. I'll fight you for it if I have to. That's the first thing I'm going to tell the lawyer."

"You won't have to. Everything's yours except half of what's in the savings and the Emerson stock."

"Isn't that generous of you. I suppose if we had kids, you'd let me have them too. You know something, Matthew? I'm glad we're childless. I'm glad I had that miscarriage nine years ago."

"You don't mean that."

"Don't I?"

"No, you don't. Hurt me if you want—don't hurt yourself."

She put her back to him, standing rigidly the way she had in the bedroom doorway. "Go on, get out of here. I can't stand to look at you. I hope to God I never see you again after today."

"You won't."

"Is that a promise?"

Cape said softly, "You'll never see me again."

"I should be so lucky."

He returned to the bedroom. His half of the closet was filled with suits, sports jackets, ties, casual clothes, a dozen pairs of shoes, a five-piece set of Gucci luggage; his dresser was jammed with shirts, underwear, socks, jewelry. Material possessions. Things. He dragged out one medium-size suitcase, filled it with essentials and one suit, two sports jackets. Took him less than fifteen minutes—just long enough to dismantle twelve years of his life.

Anna was gone when he came out again. Just as well. There was nothing more to be said.

Except one thing. And he said that aloud to the empty house, because she wouldn't have wanted to hear it anyway.

"Good-bye, Anna."

2

BERNIE Klosterman was the only one of Cape's half-dozen friends who wasn't married. He lived alone in a two-bedroom high-rise condo near downtown. Cape found him home, astonished him with the news.

"Sure, sure," Bernie said, "you can stay here tonight. Longer, if you want."

"Just tonight, thanks."

"Listen, Matt, why'd you do it? You never cheated on Anna before, did you?"

"First time."

"Taking that waitress to your house . . . man, what possessed you? If you had to bang her, why not a motel somewhere?"

"Maybe I wanted to get caught," Cape said.

Bernie stared at him. "Why would you want that?"

"The push I needed. Last push out."

"Out of the marriage? I knew the two of you weren't getting along, but—"

"Not just the marriage. Everything. Now there's no turning back."

"What're you talking about?"

"I made the date with Lonnie yesterday," Cape said. "This morning I quit my job."

"You . . . Jesus, Matt. You've been with Emerson Manufacturing, what, fourteen years? Next in line for a promotion, isn't that what you told me?"

"District sales manager, yes."

"And you quit? Just like that?"

"Just like that. I had three weeks' paid vacation coming. Gave that up in lieu of notice."

"Oh, man. They must've been pissed."

"I'm not indispensable. They won't have any trouble finding a suitable replacement. Neither will Anna."

"And what about you?"

"I told you. I'm out."

"I don't get it," Bernie said. "What does being out buy you?"

"Freedom," Cape said.

"Freedom to do what?"

"Get the hell out of Rockford, first of all."

"You mean for good?"

"For good. Burn the last bridge."

"And go where?"

"Anywhere I want. Places I've never been, things I've never seen or done. People I'd never meet if I stayed here."

"What, like a character in a Kerouac novel?"

"Not exactly, but that's the general idea. Why not?"

Bernie's expression was two-thirds incredulous, one-third disturbed. And seasoned with a touch of awe. "'Why not,' he says. This isn't the nineteen-sixties. It's a new century, and in case you haven't noticed, it's not a kinder, gentler world out there."

"I've noticed, all right. Whole damn world's gone crazy. The lunatics have finally taken over the asylum."

"Well? You can't run away from it."

"I'm not trying to."

"That's what it sounds like to me."

"I know what I'm doing," Cape said.

"Famous last words."

"You think I've gone crazy, too."

"What else can I think? Throwing away everything you've built so you can go chasing around the country looking for—what? Adventure, excitement?"

"Among other things."

"Trouble, that's what you'll find. Or disappointment or both. You're not a kid anymore, you're thirty-five years old."

"Thirty-five and stagnating. Vegetating. Suffocating."

"It can't be that bad."

"Not for you, not for most people. It is for me. Boring job, stale marriage, golf on Saturdays, poker once a month, ball game every now and then, win or lose a few bucks on the Bulls and Bears and Super Bowl, drink a few beers with the same old crowd in the same old places—that's been my entire adult life, Bernie. It's a tight little box, a trap with only one door that keeps inching down a little farther every day. And the unstable world situation only makes it that much tighter. I've got to get out now, right now, while there's still time—before the door comes down all the way. Simple as that."

"Simple, hell," Bernie said. "How're you going to live?"

"My half of our savings. Money from my Emerson stocks."

"You can't have all that much put aside."

"Enough to start with."

"What happens when it runs out?"

"Get a job, what else?"

"Sure. Lots of jobs out there for former industrial salesmen, all of them hard labor for low wages."

Cape said, "I'm not going to worry about that now. Hell, I might get lucky with cards or a horse somewhere along the line."

"Gambling? Man, if you start trying to run up your bankroll . . ."

"Easy does it. I'm not a big risk taker, you know that."

"I did until now. What do you call this scheme of yours, if not a big risk?"

"A fresh start," Cape said.

". . . You're really going through with this."

"I really am."

"Nothing else I can say, then. It's your funeral."

"Could be." Cape smiled with a corner of his mouth. "But at least I'll be alive for a while. Really alive for the first time."

"I just talked to Anna," Mary Lynn said. "My sweet Lord, Matthew. How could you have done such a wicked thing?"

Cape said nothing.

"God will punish you. You'll feel His wrath one day."

"The wages of sin," he intoned.

"That's right."

"We're all sinners, Mary Lynn. Even you."

"Yes, but my conscience is clear."

"Sure it is. Never even an impure thought, right?"

"Fornication is a mortal sin," she said. "If you don't beg God's forgiveness, you'll burn in the fires of hell."

"No sermons," Cape said. "I didn't call to listen to you thump the Bible. Any more of that, and I'll hang up on you."

"Why did you call? I can't offer you any comfort, after what you did."

"I don't know," he said.

"Don't know? Don't know why you called?"

"Predictable conversation, so far."

A baby began squalling in the background. Preschool voices rose querulously. His sister had four children, another on the way, and a husband who was overworked, submissive, and had the emotional maturity of a ten-year-old—another kid for her to handle, this one sorely in need of a vasectomy. Mary Lynn was thirty-two; she looked forty-five.

"You're just like Pop," she said.

"That's a lousy thing to say."

"It's the truth. A fornicator just like him. His drinking and fornicating sent Mama to an early grave."

"Oh, bullshit."

"Matthew. You know I can't abide that kind of language."

"Cancer killed her, not Pop."

"She might've survived if it hadn't been for his evil ways."

"All right. Have it your way."

Martyr's sigh. "Where are you?"

"Bernie Klosterman's. Just for tonight."

"Then where will you go?"

"I don't know yet."

"To confession and then home to Anna, that's where you should go. Get down on your knees and beg her to take you back."

"Beg God's forgiveness, beg Anna's forgiveness."

"Yes."

"She wouldn't take me back, no matter how much I groveled."

"She might."

"Is that what she told you?"

"Well, not in so many words . . ."

"She's all through with me. I'm not going back anyway."

"Matthew . . ."

"I'm leaving town tomorrow," Cape said. "Going away."

"Leaving Rockford? Have you lost your mind?"

"Found it. Made it up."

"My Lord, you can't just leave."

"Why can't I?"

"You have responsibilities here—Anna, your work, your family—"

"I'll take care of my responsibilities. The rest doesn't matter."

"How can you say that? Don't I matter to you? Don't Ralph and the children matter to you?"

"Yes, but I don't see any of you except on holidays. We have almost nothing in common, and you and I don't get along half the time."

"That isn't true."

"It's true. You keep trying to shove religion down my throat, everybody's throat."

"What a godless thing to say!"

"Right. Anyone who doesn't think the way you do is evil and godless."

"You sound just like Pop."

"Pop again."

"The devil's in you, Matthew, the same as he's in Pop. Consorting with harlots, blaspheming, doing Satan's work. If you don't cast him out, embrace the Almighty, you're doomed to eternal damnation—"

Cape said gently, "Good-bye, Mary Lynn," and hung up on her.

He called the old man's number in Vero Beach, Florida. Sudden impulse. Bernie went out to buy some groceries, and Cape was sitting there in the silence, and the phone caught his eye. The next second he was on his feet, using it.

An unfamiliar voice answered, saying "The Party House" in faintly slurred tones. Laughter, music, loud voices, came over the wire behind it.

"I'm calling for Sam Cape. This the right number?"

"Sure, Sam's Party House. Who're you?"

"His son. Matt."

"No kidding? Sam never said anything about having a son."

"If he's there, put him on."

"Just a minute."

The receiver banged against something on the other end. The party sounds rose and fell like a pulse. Somebody yelled, somebody else squealed, a woman said distinctly, "That Polly, she gives blow jobs a bad name." A minute passed. Then the same male voice spoke again in his ear.

"He can't come to the phone right now. Sam can't."

"Why can't he?"

Seal-bark laugh. "He's indisposed. Any message?"

"No. No message."

"Want him to call you back?"

"Forget it," Cape said. "We don't have anything to say to each other after all. Hell, we never did."

3

THE bank officer was a plump middle-aged woman with a smile that she wore like cheap perfume. She peered at her computer screen, wrote carefully on a slip of paper; tapped the keys, and wrote again. She slid the paper over to Cape's side of the desk.

"There you are, Mr. Cape. The balances in both your accounts."

He looked at the figures. Checking: $1,678.24. Savings: $26,444.75.

"Let the checking account stand," he said, "except that I want my name taken off it."

"And the savings?"

"Withdraw thirteen thousand, leave the rest. My name off that one, too."

"Ah, may I ask the reason you're—"

"No," Cape said.

She colored slightly, as much from his direct stare as from the sharp negative. She lowered her gaze a couple of inches, kept it fixed on his mouth and chin. "What would you like done with the thirteen thousand dollars?"

"Open a new checking account in my name only, deposit nine thousand. The rest of the money in cash, six hundred in fifties, four hundred in twenties."

"Yes, sir. If you'd like a new ATM card—"

"I won't need one. I've got credit cards."

She busied herself with forms. Not looking at him any longer, not saying anything, as if he were already gone.

At his brokerage firm downtown Cape put in an order to sell his shares of Emerson Manufacturing stock and deposit the proceeds in his new checking account. After transaction fees, the amount came to a little more than fourteen thousand.

Cape's car was a three-year-old brown Buick Riviera, supercharged V-6, chrome premium wheels, all the options. He'd driven it out of state only a few times, on short business trips; it had just 29,000 miles on it, was in near-new condition inside and out. He took it around to half a dozen dealerships before he found the car and the trade package he was hunting for. When he left Hammerschlag Motors, "Nobody in Illinois Beats Our Prices," he was behind the wheel of a '91 yellow-and-black Corvette, six-speed, most of the extras plus a new glass top. The odometer read 57,500, and the salesman swore it had had just one owner. Cape didn't believe either claim, but he took it anyway. It was exactly what he'd always wanted.

On his test drive it had handled reasonably well on turns and curves, smooth-shifting through all the gears, fast pickup, no pings or knocks or rough spots in the engine. Now he took it out on the interstate and opened it up to eighty-five for a mile or so on a straight stretch where the traffic was light. Blew along just fine.

He was almost ready to go.

St. Vincent's was on the south side, in the neighborhood where he'd grown up. Old neighborhood, old church: grit-darkened stone, twin steeples surmounted by bronze crosses, scrolled and brassbound entrance doors. Inside it was cool, dark, hushed. And empty this afternoon, as far as he could see.

He walked slowly down the center aisle, slid into one of the pews toward the front. He sat there with his hands on his knees. Crucified Christ gazed down on him from the wall above and behind the altar. So did the Virgin Mary, the twelve apostles at the Last Supper, other biblical scenes in bronze and backlit stained glass.

Cape stared at the altar, seeing it for a time and then not seeing it. The silence seemed to echo faintly with half-remembered voices, half-remembered words. *Dominus vobiscum. Et cum spiritu tuo. Pater noster, cui es in caelis.* Hail Mary, full of grace. Blessed art thou among women. Pray for us sinners now and at the hour of our death. *Kyrie eleison.*

For a long time he sat without moving. The restlessness stirred in him finally, brought him out of himself. On impulse he made the sign of the cross, something he hadn't done in more than a decade. Mary Lynn would have been astonished. Probably would've tried to take credit for him being here. He stood, turned out of the pew.

Someone was standing in the shadows by the nave, watching him.

Priest. Young, Cape saw as he came forward, dark-haired and moonfaced, shapeless in his robes. Smiling.

"Hello. I'm Father Zerbeck."

"Hello, Father."

"I don't believe we've met. Are you a member of this parish?"

"Once, a long time ago. I grew up three blocks from here."

"You still have family in the neighborhood?"

"Not anymore."

"Have you moved back here, then?"

"No."

"But I've seen you here before, haven't I? Recently?"

"A time or two," Cape admitted.

"May I ask why?"

"It's a good place to sit and think. Look inside yourself, make decisions."

"Is that the only reason you come to St. Vincent's?"

"I'm not much for prayer, Father."

"That's too bad," the priest said, but he was still smiling. "You seem troubled. Is there anything I can do?"

"No. My decisions are all made."

"That isn't what I meant."

"I know what you meant," Cape said.

"If you'd like to take confession—"

"I don't think so. Wouldn't do me any good."

"Are you so sure of that?"

"Sure enough."

"It's never too late to ask for God's help."

"Isn't it?"

"Have you . . . lost your faith?"

"The way you mean it, I guess I have."

"What caused you to lose it?"

"That's between God and me."

"So you do still believe in him?"

"I believe in him, all right," Cape said. "What I question is that he's as benevolent as we're taught."

"Then why do you still come to his house?"

"I told you, it's a good place to sit and think."

"Have you tried talking to him? He does listen, you know."

"I'm all talked out."

"He'll help you find yourself, if you let him."

"I'm not lost. Not anymore."

"Aren't you?" the priest said.

Cape said, "Keep the faith for both of us, Father," and went out of this cool, hushed sanctuary for the last time.

At 4:15 he was on the highway again.

Heading southwest, the radio tuned to a Chicago jazz station, the window rolled down, air rushing in hot and humid against his face.

First stop? It didn't matter.

He cranked up the volume, bore down harder on the gas.

No longer standing still.

4

ST. Louis.
   Nashville.
   Memphis.
   No set itinerary. Each new day a discovery. Interstates, state
and county highways, back roads. Large cities, small cities, rural
towns, backwaters. Tourist attractions and scenic vistas; bleak al-
leys and redneck haunts. High life, low life, day people and night
crawlers. The good, the bad, and the ugly. He wanted to taste
them all.
   Vicksburg.
   Natchez.
   Deep in the heart of Dixie. Traces of the antebellum South in
the oldest civilized settlement on the Mississippi River. Under-the-
Hill section along the waterfront; medium-stakes poker game in
one of the back rooms of a tavern that had once been a cotton storage warehouse. Five- and seven-card stud and Texas Hold'em.
He'd learned poker in his dorm at Ball State, played a fair amount
of it since. Knew the game's finer points, but had never had a great
deal of luck. Too conservative, not enough focus or concentration.
Here he found himself playing in a different style—betting aggressively, card tracking, reading the other players' faces and body language, bluffing, sandbagging, raising to the limit now and then. He

walked out eight hours later with over six hundred dollars in winnings. And a lesson learned.

Baton Rouge. Still moving south, loosely paralleling the river on its twisting path to the Gulf of Mexico.

New Orleans.

The French Quarter. Gutbucket jazz, hot and lowdown, at Preservation Hall and the smaller clubs. Street-corner hornmen in Jackson Square. Jambalaya and peppery crayfish and foaming mugs of Cajun beer. Crowds, ancient crumbling buildings, a sense of history as palpable in the sultry air as the mingled smells of beignets and fried andouille sausage, garbage and humanity and Old Man River.

On the afternoon of his third day there, Cape was walking along a relatively quiet section of Dauphine Street. Ahead was a woman in her sixties, alone, big leather bag slung over her right shoulder. As the woman passed by one of the overhanging lacework balconies, somebody jumped out of the shadows and made a lunge for the bag. Kid no more than twenty, long greasy hair, face like a pitted fox's. The woman resisted. He punched her in the face, bringing a spurt of blood, tore the bag loose, and took off running.

Cape chased him. Flash-frozen one instant, rushing ahead the next. The kid zigzagged across the street, up one block, down another. A couple of other people had seen it happen, were giving pursuit and yelling, but only Cape stayed close. The kid dodged into an alley; Cape went in after him. Halfway along, the kid stopped suddenly and swung around. A thin-bladed knife glinted in his hand.

Cape slowed, but he didn't pull up or veer off. Pure instinct kept him moving in a straight line, even when the kid made a jabbing motion with the knife. He feinted right, avoiding another jab, came back left, and knocked the knife arm out of the way. At the same time he kicked the kid squarely in the crotch.

The kid went down, squealing and writhing. Cape stepped hard on his wrist, grinding down until pain-clenched fingers opened around the knife. He kicked it out of the way. Then he threw his weight down on the skinny body, caught hold of the kid's throat, and held him like that until help arrived.

Later, one of the cops who showed up said to him, "That was a pretty brave thing you did, Mr. Cape."

"I didn't think about it, just did it."

"Still, it took a lot of guts."

Maybe so. Guts he hadn't even known he had.

Another lesson learned.

Shreveport.

Fort Smith and over into Oklahoma.

Tulsa.

Downtown, early evening, he met a man named Luther Babcock who sold religious novelties. Mini-Bibles with solid brassbound covers, standard Bibles encrusted with rhinestones and bejeweled crosses that glowed in the dark. Crucifixes containing "guaranteed genuine healing water from the world's most blessed shrine" and bearing the words "Lourdes, France" embossed in pure gold leaf; crucifixes with the entire Lord's Prayer written in miniature and a telescopic magnifying crystal in the center so you could read every word. Inspirational books, pamphlets, and videos, a life-size portrait of Jesus on gold-threaded velvet, a devotional music box that played "Amazing Grace" and two other hymns, a translucent Jesus night-light made out of ivory-colored plastic.

"The God game, my boy. Spreading the Word in small but significant ways to all the lonely sinners. A blessed profession, walking hand in hand with the angels. Enriches the spirit at the same time it enriches the pocketbook. Yessir, you do God proud, and he'll do you proud in return."

Babcock was drunk when he said it.

Five minutes afterward, he put his hand on Cape's thigh and offered to perform oral sex on him.

Back down south through Dallas, Austin, San Antonio.

Corpus Christi.

One-night stand in his Gulf-view motel room with a bonily attractive twenty-something named Kristin. Safe sex; she insisted on it. Later, Cape woke up and caught her fully dressed with his wallet in her hand. She gave him a sob story about losing her job a month ago, couldn't find another, might not be able to pay her rent. Odds-on it was either a half-truth or an outright lie, but she made it sound convincing.

He said, "Why didn't you ask for money before we went to bed? I might've paid you."

"I don't mind giving my body, but I won't sell it. No way."

"You'd rather steal?"

"I'd rather steal."

"Well, you could ask me for a loan. Now, I mean."

"Loan? That's another word for charity."

"And you don't take charity?"

"I don't beg, either."

"Funny set of ethics you have."

"Maybe," she said, "but they're mine."

There was a little better than a hundred dollars in the wallet. Cape took out all but two twenties and a ten, put the wallet back into his pants pocket. "I'm going to the bathroom," he said. "We'll talk some more after I'm done in there."

When he came out five minutes later, the wallet was empty and Kristin was gone.

Brownsville.

Across the Rio Grande to Matamoros.

Jai alai at a local *fronton*. Team and individual matches, the competitors all with single names. Fast, fast, fast game. Players leaping up and off walls, catching the little goatskin-covered hard-rubber pelota in handmade wooden baskets and hurling it off granite blocks at speeds up to 188 miles an hour. Betting on the same principle as horse racing: win, place, show; Daily Double, Trifecta, Superfecta. Plus another double called Quiniela, where you selected two players or teams to finish first and second in any order. Cape took a flyer, made a few minimum bets. Lost them all, but came close to winning a Big Q that would have paid him the equivalent of a hundred and fifty dollars.

After the jai alai, a little time in the tenderloin section along the river. Wide open. Roaming hookers, many in their teens; shills for live-sex clubs and cockfights. An old lady in a black shawl, with eyes as dead as an embalmed corpse's, offered him his choice of drugs at cut-rate prices. All this before nightfall. He went back across to U.S. soil, and what came crawling out of the hot, neon-spattered Tex-Mex night in the tenderloin over there wasn't any better.

Not for him. Tasting sin was one thing. Wallowing in it was something else entirely.

North again. Lubbock, Amarillo.

West then into New Mexico, following what was left of the old Route 66. Tucumcari, Santa Rosa, Albuquerque.

Another backroom poker game. Bad run of cards that aggressive play couldn't overcome. Down and out three hundred in less than four hours. Easy come, easy go.

Santa Fe.

Over into Arizona, through the Painted Desert, down to Flagstaff.

Phoenix.

Air show out on the desert, biplanes and other vintage aircraft, barnstorming wing walkers and a variety of aerobatics. In line at one of the booths selling beer he got into a conversation with a sinewy, leather-brown woman who turned out to be a skydiver. Yvonne. Before the show ended, she invited him to go up and jump with her and some friends the next day.

All his life Cape had been acrophobic. On a plane just twice, commercial flights, both unavoidable business trips and both requiring alcohol anaesthesia. He grinned lopsidedly at Yvonne and said without hesitation, "Sure, why not?"

They went up at noon, five divers and a pilot in a big Beechcraft. Yvonne fed Cape the do's and don'ts, an hour's worth of indoctrination that centered on his parachute. He froze up a little when they opened the door. Other than that, he managed it all right. Kept his eyes open when he jumped, counted slowly to ten before he pulled the rip cord, worked the lines the way he'd been told. The whole thing was a fear-and-adrenaline high, all except the landing. He came down awkwardly and a little too hard, bounced and rolled, and ended up with half a dozen bruises. Even so, the others were full of congratulations. Yvonne had something else for him, all that night and the next morning. Diving made her horny as hell, she said.

Cape spent a week with her. Went diving twice more, longer freefalls and bigger highs. The third time, he stood in the open door with the wind screaming in his ears and looked down through three thousand feet of nothing at a checkerboard landscape. No fear before or after he jumped; and the high was all adrenaline. Just like that, he wasn't afraid of heights any longer.

Prescott.

The Grand Canyon and Hoover Dam.

Las Vegas.

Heat, smog, desert sprawl, the longest downtime traffic lights in the country. The Strip didn't impress him. Glitter and glitz and money-worshiping, sugarcoated, bleary-eyed craziness; people swarming over everything like brightly colored ants over piles of rock candy. Cape spent minutes inside New York, New York, just long enough to see what a Vegas pleasure palace was like. Then he headed for one of the downscale strip joints a few miles away.

He lasted twenty minutes in there, paying forty dollars to find out what a nude lap dance was all about. Another taste of corruption that wasn't for him, neither the joint nor the dance. Demeaning to the women, demeaning to him, if not to the other panting and sweating male customers.

That night, two guys tried to break into the Corvette in the parking lot outside his motel room. They set the alarm off, and by the time Cape got out there, groggy with sleep, they were shadows disappearing into deeper shadows. Their jimmying had damaged the door so that it would no longer shut tightly, but at least he could still lock it. Scratches in the paint, too, not that they amounted to much. The 'Vette hadn't been a virgin when he married her.

He left Vegas at dawn.

Vegas was a gaudily disguised trap, a sugared slice of hell, no better underneath than the Tex-Mex tenderloins. Leaving it was like an escape.

Death Valley.

Some people might call it a slice of hell, too, but he wasn't one of them. Awe-inspiring. Stark vistas, vast brown and gray and salt-white emptiness, bare jagged mountains brooding all around. Dazzling sunlight, ink-black shadows. So still the silence hurt your ears. You stood looking out from Zabriskie Point, or one of the high spots in the Grapevines and Panamints, and it put everything into perspective. You understood that you really didn't matter much, alive or dead. That nobody did. That this place had been here for millions of years, and would be here for millions more after you were gone. The knowledge was somehow comforting.

Barstow.

Palm Springs.

Los Angeles.

Beach scene for a day. Didn't appeal to him much. Phony, superficial, everybody playing a role—surfer, beach bum, bikini bombshell—like extras in a bad teenage movie.

The rest of L.A. was clogged freeways, towns that weren't towns but teeming highway connectors, smog so thick the sky was yellow-brown and breathing hurt your throat and lungs and screwed up your sinuses.

Two days of California Dreaming, and he was on the road again.

Santa Barbara. Better, but still too much residual L.A.

Big Sur on Highway 1. Much, much better. The air, the coastline, the Pacific Ocean—all clean, beautiful, unspoiled.

Carmel. Monterey.

Argument in a pool parlor with a local who tried to hustle him. Nothing came of it inside, but later, when Cape left, the local and one of his buddies jumped him on the street. Wasn't much of a fight; they were both too drunk to do any real damage. But they kept trying to get his wallet away from him, and that made him furious. He smashed the hustler's nose, stomped the other one's hand, left them both down and moaning, and drove off before anybody else showed up. The last thing he wanted was trouble with the law.

The fight stayed with him that night, into the next day. The depth of his anger, the capacity for violence—he didn't like that hidden side of himself. He would have to be careful to keep it caged. Still, there was cold comfort in knowing that if he needed it, had to depend on it in a tight spot, it was a coiled and powerful part of him.

San Francisco.

And in San Francisco, he met Tanya and Boone Judson.

5

H E bumped into her in the ornate lobby of the Sir Francis Drake. Literally. He came wandering in there; the marbled and muraled expanse was crowded with people wearing badges, somebody yacking and not paying attention stepped into his path, he veered to avoid collision and had one anyway. They caromed off each other, not hard. She smiled ruefully; he did a small double take.

In that first quick glance he thought she was Anna.

Same long, lean body type. Blond hair cut short and side-swept across the forehead. Hollowed cheekbones, wide mouth, green eyes. He blinked—and she wasn't Anna anymore. Younger, her skin browner, the eyes more hazel than green, neck longer, ears set more closely against her skull. The resemblance, once he'd gotten a good look, was no more than superficial.

She looked at him looking at her, head cocked quizzically to one side. "You think you know me?" she asked.

Cape said, "No. Sorry," and stepped around and away from her. He made his way through the crowd into the lobby bar. Small and packed solid. He came back out again. A billboard wall sign caught his eye: STARLITE ROOF, and the words "Dining, Dancing, Cocktails." He'd come into the hotel looking for a drink; he didn't want to go out and look someplace else. He rode one of the elevators up to the Starlite Roof.

Big rambling room in the same Renaissance style as the lobby, ringed with tall windows that provided sweeping views of the city and the Bay. Not nearly as many people here: early yet, a little after four. Cape found an empty table, ordered Jack Daniel's on the rocks. He'd spent most of the day walking around North Beach, Chinatown, the downtown area. Tired now, and his back ached. He needed some downtime as much as he needed the drink.

He'd been there about five minutes when the blond woman walked in. Alone. She stood glancing around the room; her gaze touched him, lingered briefly, moved on. There was one window table left, and she claimed it. Male eyes followed her across the room, Cape's among them. She had that kind of figure, that kind of bearing.

Cape sipped his drink, admiring the cityscape. When his attention shifted, he caught the blond peering his way. It happened again, twice. The third time he quit watching the view, watched her instead. She brushed off two men who came to her table. Her drink was something dark with fruit in it; she worked on that for a while. Then her head came up, and she was looking at him again.

He got up and carried his drink over there. Nothing in her expression welcomed him. Cool, aloof. He said, "You think you know *me?*"

It wasn't what she expected. The edges of her mouth twitched upward. "I guess I was staring, at that."

"Payback for downstairs? Or some other reason?"

"Not the kind you're thinking."

"How do you know what I'm thinking?"

"You're a man, aren't you?"

"Not all men are the same."

"They are in my experience. I'm not looking for company."

"Then why the long-distance appraisal?"

"I suppose because of the way you looked at me in the lobby. It made me curious. *Do* I remind you of somebody?"

"Superficially. My soon-to-be-ex wife."

"Oh. I see."

"I don't think you do," Cape said.

"Not carrying a torch? Well."

"Is it all right if I sit down?"

"I told you, I'm not looking for company. As a matter of fact, I'm waiting for someone."

"Husband, boyfriend?"

"It might not be a man, you know."

"With you, I'll bet it usually is."

Two-thirds of a smile this time. "I thought I'd heard all the lines. That one's not bad."

"You didn't answer my question."

"I really am waiting for someone."

"If it's your husband, I'll go away quietly."

"I'm not married," she said.

"Fiancé? Lover?"

"My brother."

Cape waited, one eyebrow raised interrogatively.

"Well, all right," she said. "Just until Boone gets here."

He sat down. The afternoon sunlight slanting in through the windows showed tawny flecks in her hazel eyes. Cat's eyes, frank and direct.

"My name's Matt. Short for Matthew."

"Matthew what?"

"Cape."

She said immediately, deadpan, "Hatteras or Kennedy?"

It wasn't funny, but he laughed anyway.

"Tanya Judson."

"Interesting name. Tanya."

"My mother's family were White Russians." She sipped her drink. "You don't look like you belong here, Matt."

"No? How do I take that?"

"I mean," she said, "you're not wearing a badge. I take it you're not part of the convention."

"What convention is that?"

"Million Dollar Round Table. Insurance agents who've written a million dollars or more worth of business."

"Not hardly. Is that why you're here?"

"Yes and no. I'm not a Round Table agent, but Boone is. My brother."

"And you're his date for this convention?"

"His wife couldn't get time off from her job. I happen to like San Francisco. So yes, you could say I'm his date."

"No trouble getting time off from your job?"

"I'm a computer graphics designer. Freelance."

"Not married, you said."

"I was, once. First, last, and only time."

"That bad?"

"That bad. And don't ask me if I'm involved with anyone or how I feel about short-term relationships. The answers don't concern you."

"Then why let me sit down?"

"I'm easily bored. And you seem like you might be interesting to talk to for a while."

"Uh-huh. As long as the conversation doesn't get too personal."

"Intelligent, too. Another point in your favor."

Cape nibbled sour mash. "Where do you and your brother live?"

"San Diego. Where do you live?"

"At the moment, a motel on Lombard Street."

"I meant—"

"I'm from the Midwest," he said, "but I don't live there anymore. I don't live anywhere anymore. Here a while, there a while."

"Ah. Drifter."

"Road warrior. Sounds better."

"How long have you been living that kind of life?"

"Not long enough."

"You must have money. Or do you just move from job to job?"
He shrugged.

"Or maybe you rob banks in your spare time?"

"Too dangerous."

"I know—you're a professional gambler. You've got that steely-eyed look."

"Wrong. But I wouldn't mind being one."

"Why do you say that?"

"Gambling's an interest of mine."

"Really? You do much of it?"

"Now and then," Cape said.

"Good enough at it to make a living?"

"Don't I wish. I lose as often as I win."

"Blackjack, roulette?"

"Poker, mainly. That's my game."

Tanya smiled and then laughed.

"What's funny?"

"Well, it so happens— Oh, here's Boone. I'll let him tell you."

The man who came up to the table was about Cape's age. Round-faced, on the pudgy side, losing his dust-colored hair on both sides of a long centerpiece like a skinny peninsula in a pink sea. Conservatively dressed: blue suit with a convention badge pinned to the coat pocket, white shirt, blue-and-white silk tie. He didn't look much like Tanya. Except for the smile he wore: sunny, showing a lot of white teeth.

"Sorry I'm late, kiddo," he said to Tanya. He ran liquidy, bright blue eyes over Cape as if he were examining a plate of unfamiliar food. "Who's your friend?"

She introduced them. "Matt's not with the convention," she said.

"Figured that," Boone said cheerfully. "No badge. You're lucky, Matt, you don't got to wear no stinking badge."

"That's right. I'm lucky."

"Local? Or visitor like us?"

"He's a road warrior," Tanya said.

"A which?"

"His home is the open road."

"Oh, a free spirit. Now I really think you're a lucky guy, Matt. Wish I could live that kind of life instead of being tied down to a nine-to-five."

"You seem to be doing pretty well at your nine-to-five."

"Can't complain, can't complain."

Tanya said, "Matt was just telling me he likes to gamble."

"Is that right?"

"Guess what his game is?"

"Not poker?"

"Poker," she said, and Boone laughed with her this time.

Cape said, "How about letting me in on the joke?"

"Not a joke, just a funny coincidence." She laid cool fingertips on the back of Cape's hand. "My dear brother happens to be a poker nut himself. He also happens to be getting up a game tonight. You haven't filled all the seats yet, have you, Boone?"

"One left," Boone said. "Interested, Matt?"

"Depends. Where and when?"

"My suite at the Conover Arms. That's a couple of blocks away, on Geary—we couldn't get in here at the Drake. Nine o'clock."

"What kind of poker?"

"Stud and draw. Keep it simple, that's my motto."

"Wild cards?"

Boone looked offended. "No way. I hate wild-card games."

"So do I. Stakes?"

"Table stakes. Five-dollar ante, twenty-dollar limit, no limit on raises."

"How many players?"

"A full seven, if you'll join us."

Cape asked Tanya, "Will you be playing?"

"Me? God, no. Boone's the only gambler in our family."

"That's too bad."

"I'm sure you think so." Her smile held mock sympathy.

"The others are all conventioneers like me," Boone said. "Dilettantes bit by the gambling bug, you might say." He paused, measuring Cape again with his liquidy gaze. "Strictly a friendly game."

"No sharks allowed."

"No, sir, no sharks allowed."

"Suits me. I like swimming in safe waters myself."

Boone beamed at him. "Count you in for the last seat, then?"

"Count me in."

6

BOONE Judson's two-room suite at the Conover Arms was on the small side—just enough space in the sitting room for an oblong table and eight chairs provided by the hotel staff. The lighting was weak, two lamps and a ceiling globe. On the table: wheel carrier of red, white, and blue chips and four sealed decks of blue-backed Bicycle cards. On a sideboard: plenty of liquor, ice, snack food.

"Only thing we haven't got," Boone said through his sunny smile, "is naked babes. You gents'll have to make those arrangements for yourselves."

Everybody laughed, Cape included. Five of them there now, just before nine o'clock, clustered around the sideboard waiting for the last two players to show up. Drinks in hand, chattering, eager to get started. The conventioneers drank Scotch or bourbon; Cape drank plain soda over ice. They accepted him anyway. He knew how to blend in with salesmen; he'd been one himself for too many years, gone to his share of conventions. Memorize names and hometowns, use them often. Joke, glad-hand, pretend interest in dull banter. Drop names like Emerson Manufacturing into the conversation.

The last two insurance agents trooped in twenty minutes later, half in the bag and spouting excuses. Everybody got acquainted, freshened drinks. Then they took seats at random around the table.

"Virgin decks, boys," Boone said. "Matt, you do the honors. Pick one and pop its cherry."

Cape slit the cellophane, broke the seal, shook the cards free, and removed the jokers. He gave the deck seven or eight hard shuffles to take out some of the stiff newness. Dealt one card to everybody, face up. Scott from Cleveland caught a deuce and grumbled about it; banking would interfere with his concentration, he said, as if the liquor he was knocking back wouldn't. He was one of the latecomers.

Buy-in was five hundred. Cape took the minimum. Most of the others took a thousand, and Joe from St. Louis laid out fifteen crisp hundred-dollar bills. Fat wallets, all the way around the table.

The play started off slow, on the conservative side, the way the bigger-money games among strangers usually do. Feeling one another out. Cape paid particular attention to a different man through each of the first six hands—faces, eyes, body language, the way he held his cards, when he bet and how much and how often, if and when he folded. Mitch from East Rutherford looked to be the strongest player. Scott from Cleveland and Charley from Seattle were scatterguns, more interested in drinking and yacking than working at their games. Boone was the hardest to read—loose but casual, not drinking much, folding quickly unless he had the cards to back up a bet, raising only once. The sandbagging, check-and-raise type.

It was forty minutes before Cape won a small pot. Another thirty minutes before he won a second. Bad cards again, the kind of streak you had to just ride out. The play had picked up by then—larger bets, a couple of pots that exceeded three hundred each. Winners so far were Mitch from East Rutherford and Boone, who claimed both of the three-hundred-plus pots: kings full in a hand of draw dealt by Charley from Seattle, trip aces in five-card stud dealt by Joe from St. Louis.

Cape lost slowly but steadily. His buy-in five hundred was gone in less than two hours; another five hundred went even faster. Scott from Cleveland, Charley from Seattle, and Perry from Sarasota were even bigger losers. Mitch from East Rutherford kept winning. So did Boone. Four or five medium-size pots, another fat one that Cape dropped out of halfway through the betting. He figured his three queens wouldn't be enough, and he was right.

Boone had an ace-high spade flush to Charley-from-Seattle's small straight.

"Boone," Charley said, "you're just plain-ass lucky. Drop-dead gorgeous woman like Tanya for a sister, and here you win all the big pots."

Perry from Sarasota said dreamily, "Amen on both counts."

Boone said, grinning, "Hell, if I was really lucky, I'd win every pot and Tanya'd be my wife instead of my sister."

Everybody laughed except Cape.

Not long after midnight, Charley from Seattle quit the game. He was sloppy drunk by then and down better than twenty-four hundred, by Cape's count. Forty minutes later there were just five of them; Perry from Sarasota cashed out at around nineteen hundred in the hole. Mitch from East Rutherford began to lose a little; Joe from St. Louis began to win a little. Scott from Cleveland kept throwing good money after bad, drinking Scotch and bitching the whole time; he was into the game for four thousand by then. Cape's losses were close to fifteen hundred. Boone remained the heavy winner.

Biggest pot of the night came at one-thirty, on a hand of seven-card stud dealt by Joe from St. Louis. Cape caught wired aces in the hole, a pair of sevens faceup and a third seven on his last down card. Mitch from East Rutherford had three hearts showing, and the way he bet after his last down card, he had two more hearts buried. Scott from Cleveland stayed in for a while with what was probably trips. Boone was the fourth man in; he had a pair of fours showing, nothing else.

They went back and forth, raising, Boone bumping every time. Scott from Cleveland dropped out. Mitch from East Rutherford showed less and less confidence in his heart flush, finally dropped out too.

"Just you and me, Matt," Boone said cheerfully. "Raise you another twenty."

Cape raised him back, got another raise in return. "All right," he said. He slid his last white chip into the pot. "Call."

Boone flipped over two of his hole cards. "Four times four."

"Yeah. What I figured."

"Your pot if you got more sevens hidden there."

"Just a boat full of losers. It's yours."

"Whoo-ee." Boone grinned all over his chubby face, began raking in the chips. "This really is my night. I haven't had the cards run this hot for me in years."

Cape slid his hand together, picked it up, made as if to toss it onto the fan of other discards. Instead, leaning back slightly, he let his elbow bang against the edge of the table and the cards slide from his fingers into his lap, off onto the floor. He said as if he were annoyed with himself, "Dammit, I can't do anything right tonight," and scraped his chair back.

When he hunched over and leaned down, he did two things. The ace of diamonds was still in his lap; he palmed it with his left hand. With his right he picked up one of the sevens and bent it nearly in half. "Shit!" he said as he straightened. "Now look what I did." He tossed the bent seven onto the table a couple of seconds before he dropped the remaining five cards onto the discard pile. The others looked at the damaged seven; their faces said they didn't notice the missing ace.

"Hey, don't worry about it," Boone said. "No harm done. We still got one more virgin deck."

Cape played two hands with the new deck, losing both. On the third deal he folded a pair of jacks and said, "I've got to take a leak. Deal me out of the next one."

In the bathroom, with the door locked, he took the diamond ace out of his pocket and held it up to the bright fluorescent light above the sink. He studied the front, turned it over, and studied the back. Then he tucked the card into his wallet, went back out to the table.

The five of them played for another ten minutes, Cape folding all but the last hand. He had just enough chips to make one bet, one raise, on his pair of kings. When Boone bumped him, he folded again. He was down exactly seventeen hundred.

"That's it for me," he said.

A few seconds later Joe from St. Louis lost yet another pot to Boone. He threw his cards down in disgust. "I'm done, too. Just not my night."

"Same here," Scott from Cleveland said. "Christ, I gotta be close to four thousand in the crapper."

"Get it back tomorrow night," Boone said. "My run of luck can't hold, and yours is bound to change."

"Uh-uh. Wife finds out how much I lost already . . ."

"You win it back, she'll never know, right?" Boone looked at Cape. "How about you, Matt? You want to try goosing Lady Luck again tomorrow night?"

"I'll keep it in mind."

"Do that. If you decide to play, give me a ring and I'll make sure you have a seat. If not . . . well, it's been a pleasure."

"Has it?"

"Sure. For me so far." He laughed. "No kidding, I hope you can make it. Really like to see you again."

"You will," Cape said. "You can bet on it."

7

CAPE rattled knuckles on the door marked 407. Not loud—it was close to 3:00 A.M. by his watch—but steadily, in a low staccato beat. In less than a minute he got a wary response.

"Who is it?"

He said, "Hotel security," in a voice pitched differently than his own.

No response for a time. Then, "It's the middle of the night. What do you want?"

"Security matter. Open the door, please."

"Not until you tell me what you want."

"In private, Miss Judson. Don't make me use my passkey. Or call the city police."

After that, she didn't have much choice. The chain jangled, and she released the deadbolt.

As soon as the door cracked inward, Cape laid his shoulder against it and shoved. She backpedaled, off balance, cursing. He went in and shut the door behind him.

"You," she said, spitting the word as she recognized him. "You son of a bitch, what's the idea?"

This room was a large single, with a shallow entrance foyer. The bedside lamp was lit, and the TV was on low volume, some movie with sappy music and a woman weeping. Tanya wore a lime-green silk robe, knee-length and gap-necked. With her make-up scrubbed off and her blond hair rumpled, she looked about nineteen.

She backed up near the bed, saying, "Come near me, and I'll scream the house down. You won't have enough time to yank it out, much less get it up."

"Don't flatter yourself. That's not why I'm here."

"Then what the hell do you want?"

"Seventeen hundred dollars."

". . . What?"

"You heard me. That's how much I lost tonight. Correction— that's how much you and Boone stole from me tonight."

"I don't have a clue what you're talking about."

"Sure you do. The poker con the two of you are running."

"Con? What do you mean, con?"

"He's the jolly mechanic, you're the sexpot roper and steerer. Insurance agent and graphic artist, hell. Couple of grifters working the convention circuit."

"You're crazy. Or high on something."

"I'll bet the local cops won't think so."

Nothing changed in her expression. Poker face as practiced as Boone's. She wasn't new at the game; seasoned veteran at twenty-five or so. "If you think you've been cheated, why didn't you call the police?"

"Too much hassle. I don't have the time for it."

"Don't tell me you're wanted?"

"I won't, because I'm not."

"You say anything to Boone, the other players?"

"No. Same reason I didn't notify hotel security or the city law. My freedom's more important to me than putting a couple of scam artists out of commission."

"Why come here, then? I suppose the night clerk told you where to find me."

"Bellboy. He thinks you're a stone fox."

"Fuck the bellboy. Where's Boone? My God, you didn't do anything to him?"

"Not yet. He's probably counting the take right now."

"You just want your money back, is that it?"

"That's it."

"And how much more?"

"Nothing more, not for me," Cape said. "The other five marks get theirs back, too—that's the second part of the deal."

"What deal?"

"Me keeping my mouth shut, letting the two of you off the hook."

"They all lost except Boone, is that what you're saying?"

"Lost big, a couple of them."

"I don't believe he cheated any of you. My brother's honest, you can't prove otherwise."

"Can't I?"

"I know how he plays poker. Brand-new sealed decks, and the deal passes every hand. How could he cheat six men in that kind of game?"

"Marked cards," Cape said.

"Using sealed decks? That's impossible."

He took the ace of diamonds from his wallet, showed it to her. "I palmed this from one of those sealed decks. It's marked, all right. I checked to make sure. What's known as shade work, right?"

Openmouthed stare.

"Let's see if I've got the gaff right," Cape said. "What you do is buy some decks of Bicycle cards, one of the most common brands. Blue-backs or red-backs, either one. You open the cellophane wrapper along the bottom of the box, taking care not to damage the manufacturer's stamp on top. Slide the box out, use a razor blade to pry the glued flaps apart along one side. Then dilute blue or red aniline dye with alcohol until you've got the lightest possible tint, wash it over the red or blue portion of each card back with a camel's-hair brush—tinting the white part just enough in different spots so you can see the shading if you know it's there. How am I doing so far?"

Tanya kept on staring at him, not saying anything. The poker face had begun to lose a little of its passivity.

"Once you've got all the cards marked, you put them back in the box and reseal the flaps with rubber cement. Slip the box back into the cellophane sleeve, refold the sleeve ends along the original creases, and reseal them with a drop of glue. Do the job right, nobody can tell the package has been tampered with. Then when you get up a game, you make sure one of your vics opens the sealed deck. You also make sure the lighting isn't too good so nobody can spot the shading on the cards except you."

She said, "Jesus. How did you—?"

"I told you at the Drake, I've always been interested in gambling. I also read a lot."

She sat down on the bed next to the nightstand. "You mind if I have a cigarette?" Without waiting for an answer, she reached out to open the nightstand drawer.

Cape was across the room in five long, fast strides. He caught her wrist just as her hand came out of the drawer, twisted it, and made her yell and relax her grip. He wrenched the gun out of her fingers, backed away quickly to avoid the kick she launched at him.

"You son of a bitch!"

"You already called me that. Try a new one."

She rubbed her wrist, panting a little. "I wouldn't give you the satisfaction."

Cape looked at the gun. Flat, lightweight automatic, toy-size. The safety was off; he put it on and managed to eject the clip. Five cartridges, a full load. Damn deadly toy.

Before he dropped it into his jacket pocket, he said, "What were you going to do? Shoot me for a prowler?"

"No."

"Threaten me?"

"Something like that."

"It wouldn't have worked."

Tanya shrugged, watching him through lowered lids. She was sitting on the edge of the bed, knees together, the folds of her robe drawn across her thighs. She drew back slightly, parting her legs so the robe fell away. Underneath she was naked. Slowly she lifted one leg, crossed it over the other. Sharon Stone in *Basic Instinct*.

He gave her a mirthless grin. "That won't work either."

"What won't?"

"First you try bluffing, then the gun, now sex. I'm not interested."

"I could make you interested."

"Before tonight you might have. Not anymore."

The hazel eyes dissected him. She shrugged again, pulled the robe back over her legs.

"Now what?" she said.

"Now we wait."

"For what?"

"For Boone to show up."

"What makes you think he's coming here?"

"Same thing that makes me think he's not your brother."

A key scraped in the lock at a quarter to four. Cape was slouched in an armchair to the right of the shallow entrance foyer, so he couldn't be seen from the doorway. Tanya was on the bed, propped up against the pillows, pretending he wasn't there at all.

Boone came in, saw her, and said, "Good, you're awake. Score was better than we hoped, close to sixteen thousand—"

"Seventeen hundred of it mine," Cape said.

Boone, coming through the archway, carrying a small black satchel like a doctor's bag, stopped as if he'd walked into a wall. His head swiveled jerkily; his eyes bugged a little. The smile he'd been wearing slipped, and he had difficulty pulling it back up.

He said, "Matt. Jesus, you gave me a jolt there." He glanced at Tanya, put his eyes on Cape again. "What're you doing here?"

"He spotted the gaff," Tanya said.

The smile slipped all the way off this time. Boone's round cheeks had been flushed; the color began to fade, leaving splotches of whiteness like cottage cheese curds. "What gaff?" he said. "Listen, I don't know what you think you—"

"The shade work," Cape said. "Quit trying to bluff. It didn't work for her, either."

A little silence. Then Boone squared his shoulders, drew himself up—little man trying to make himself big again. "Well. All right, then. I don't see any cops, so what is it you want?"

"He wants the money," Tanya said.

"Sure, no problem. How much was it you lost, Matt?"

"*All* the money. So he can give it back to the other marks."

"No," Boone said.

Cape said, "Yes. Put the satchel on the table over here."

Boone clutched it more tightly. He said without turning his head, "Tanya."

"I don't have the gun. He's got it."

"Goddamn it!"

"Put the satchel on the table," Cape said.

"You don't understand. This money—we need it. We'll cut you in for a percentage, say five thousand, but we've got to have the rest."

"Why?"

"Seed money, that's why."

"For what? Another con?"

"We have to be in Tahoe day after tomorrow—"

"Shut up, Boone," Tanya said.

"Six thousand," Boone said to Cape. "That's as high as we can go."

"Put the satchel on the table."

"No. Matt, will you just listen—"

Cape took the little automatic out of his pocket. "One more time. Put the satchel on the table."

Boone obeyed finally. He took a couple of sideways steps, jammed the bag down hard enough so that the two top halves parted like a gaping mouth. He didn't look soft and pudgy any longer; he looked small and hard and swollen with corruption. Boone the boil, ready to pop.

"You won't get away with this," he said between his teeth. "This is my goddamn money!"

"*Our* goddamn money," Tanya said bitterly.

"Take it away, and you'll regret it, Matt. Guaranteed."

Cape got to his feet. "Go over and sit on the bed with your wife or girlfriend or whatever she is."

"You think I'd marry him?" she said. "A little toad like him?"

"Now *you* shut the fuck up, Tanya. This is all your fault. Why'd you let him in here? Why'd you let him get hold of your gun?"

She just looked at him, a faint sneer on her mouth.

"I ought to break your neck."

"Try it and see what it gets you."

"On the bed," Cape said again, gesturing with the automatic. "Go on."

Glaring, Boone went over and sat down apart from the woman.

Cape picked up the black bag. "I wouldn't try setting up another game tomorrow night, if I were you. In fact, I'd be a long way from San Francisco by then. Word's going to get around when I return this money."

"Go to hell."

"If I do, maybe the three of us can play poker with the devil."

Boone and Tanya both had something to say to that, but their angry voices commingled, and he didn't pay much attention anyway. He was already on his way out of there with the satchel.

8

CAPE made sure the blinds were tightly closed, then upended the satchel over the motel-room bed. Packets of rumpled green, a dozen or so, loosely held together with rubber bands. Something else, too: a nine-by-twelve manila envelope, mostly flat, closed but not sealed.

The money first. Six packets of hundreds, three of fifties, two thicker ones of twenties, another of tens, fives, and singles. He made a riffling count without removing any of the rubber bands. Eighteen thousand and change. The night's score was around sixteen thousand, by Cape's estimate and Boone's announcement on entering Tanya's room. The remaining two thousand belonged to the grifters—seed money to grow a bigger crop of seed money.

He fed the cash back into the satchel, opened the manila envelope. Photographs. Four eight-by-ten color glossies. Two of them were candid shots of the same woman, taken at relatively close range; the angles and her expression said she hadn't known she was being photographed. Sleek, big-eyed, tawny hair worn long enough to caress the swell of her breasts, some kind of beauty mark at one corner of a broad-lipped mouth. In one snap she was dressed in an expensive cream-colored outfit and getting into a silver BMW. In the other she wore a pale yellow sundress and was standing in front of the purple-and-gold entrance to what appeared to be a hotel-casino complex. Part of a name was visible in the background, the words LAK and GRAND.

The other two photos were studio portraits of men. One: sixty-ish, distinguished looking, flowing silver mustache and wavy silver hair. The other: around forty, olive-toned skin, curly black hair, handsome in a slick, hard way, eyes like fragments of black ice.

Cape looked at the backs of the glossies. Nothing written on any of them. He checked the envelope again, examined the satchel inside and out. Nothing. He put the photos inside with the money, set the satchel on the nightstand.

The digital alarm clock read 5:10 when he finally crawled into bed.

Edges of daylight and street noise woke him. Nine-fifteen. Four hours' sleep, but he didn't want much more than that. Downtime was lost time; each night's rest was one less place to see, one less thing to do.

Before he left the room, he wrapped Tanya's little automatic in a plastic clothes bag from the closet. Outside he hunted up the motel's Dumpster, tossed the bag in. The satchel he locked in the 'Vette's trunk.

Breakfast in a nearby coffee shop. Then he drove around the neighborhood until he found a chain drugstore large enough to have a stationery section. He bought five self-sealing padded mailing bags and a black marking pen.

Back in his room, he sat down with a couple of sheets of motel stationery and worked his memory. Names, faces, numbers—the salesman's stock-in-trade. Over the years he'd developed an almost total recall in all three categories. It didn't take him long to sort out and set down the loss amounts of the other five vics at last night's game, starting with their buy-in figures. Then he divided by six the two thousand that no longer belonged to Boone and Tanya, added those amounts to the individual totals. That ensured that everybody, himself included, would not only get his money back but make a small profit for his trouble.

Once he had the final figures, he opened the satchel and counted out the money into six piles. His cut he stuffed into his wallet; the others went into the five mailing bags. He considered writing some kind of note to go with the cash, but he'd have to write it five times—too much work. Unnecessary, besides. The smarter ones would figure it out for themselves, even if they never knew for sure who their benefactor was. The others wouldn't care. Free ride on a gift horse.

With the marking pen he wrote their full names on each of the bags and then sealed them. Fifteen minutes later he was checked out and on his way downtown again.

The desk clerk at the Conover Arms said, "The Judsons are no longer with us—checked out early this morning. No forwarding address, I'm afraid."

"Not a problem," Cape said. "I know where they're going."

Three of the five insurance agents were staying at the Sir Francis Drake. Cape dropped off their money first, requesting that the packages be kept in the hotel safe until claimed. The clerk there didn't ask any questions. Neither did the one manning the desk at the Hilton, the overflow convention hotel nearby where the other two players were booked.

When he was done, he picked up the 'Vette and got directions to the Bay Bridge from the parking garage attendant. Half an hour later he was on the other side of the bay, on Highway 80 headed east.

The High Sierra.

Highway 50 now, the long, steep descent from Echo Summit.

Cape pulled off onto an overlook, got out, and stood squinting into the cool mountain wind. Lake Tahoe Basin spread out below, part of the lake a bright blue blot in the distance. White-rimmed peaks, vast stretches of evergreens, massive juts and scarps of bare rock. Rugged beauty, harsh wilderness. Somewhere off to the north, where Highway 80 crested the Sierras on its asphalt path to Reno, was Emigration Gap—the place where the Donner Party had been trapped and perished, and the still living had fed briefly on the dead.

Behind him cars and trucks hissed by in a steady stream. He stayed there like that for a long time, hunched against the force of the wind, focused on the far reaches.

Up high like this, standing alone with your back to civilization, you felt that your humanity was safe.

Down below, among the roaming herds, where you couldn't tell the weak from the strong, the predators from the prey, you had to be damn careful not to become one of the cannibals yourself.

9

LAKE Tahoe.

Massive, sun-spattered, placid. Cupped by mountains all around, its far shores obscured by a bluish haze. Pleasure craft and paddlewheel excursion boats skimming like waterbugs over its surface.

South Lake Tahoe.

Not much of a town. Most of it stretched out along Lake Tahoe Boulevard, following the curve of the lakeshore. Malls, strip malls, wedding chapels, winter and summer resort businesses, a big new ski tram leading up to the flanking mountain. The last mile or so at the eastern end, it became a gamblers' town, with strings of medium-priced motels lining the road, offering gambling-related specials.

Stateline.

On the Nevada side, a short strip of high-rise casino hotels. Harrah's, Harvey's, Horizon, Bill's, Caesar's Tahoe, Lakeside Grand. Huge marquee signs advertising entertainment, come-on promotions, nonstop action—the usual ballyhoo. Mini Las Vegas, poor man's Las Vegas. A place for a quick visit, an even quicker getaway.

Cape parked in the free lot behind the Lakeside Grand. The side entrance to the hotel was the one in the photo background, all right. He pushed through into a purple-and-gold lobby ringed with boutiques and specialty shops. Crossed that and entered the casino. Mirror-walled and -ceilinged, the usual banks of neon-lit electronic slots and gaming tables presided over by people dressed in purple and gold. The slots and blackjack layouts were getting some late-afternoon play; the craps, roulette, and baccarat tables were quiet. The high rollers, like vampires, only came out at night.

He wandered through the casino, showing the eight-by-ten glossies to a woman in one of the change booths, a sleepy-eyed croupier, an equally bored stickman. Head shakes and negatives. He entered the bar at the opposite end. The purple-shirted barman said, "Can't help you, sir. Unless it's a drink you want."

A drink was just what he wanted. But not yet. He took the photos into the hotel lobby. A tour group had just come in; all the people behind the reception desk were busy. Cape crossed carpeting as thick as new sod to the shops. Jewelry, objets d'art, Asian antiques, men's and women's clothing. One of the boutiques was called Milady's Pleasure. Nobody in there now except a saleswoman in a gold blouse and purple slacks.

She said, "My name is Justine. How may I help you? A gift for milady?"

Tall, jet-black hair, pale skin, striking almond-shaped eyes. Eurasian, probably. About his age. Not beautiful, not even pretty by any conventional standard, but with the kind of features you'd remember long after one of the plastic-faced Hollywood clones. Those eyes, especially.

She was used to being scrutinized; neither her gaze nor her smile wavered. At length Cape shook his head, said through his salesman's smile, "Actually, I'm looking for someone. I wonder if you might be able to help."

"Well . . ."

He held up one of the photos of the tawny-haired woman. "Do you know her?"

"Oh . . . yes, that's Mrs. Vanowen."

"Vanowen."

"She's a customer of ours."

"Lives around here, then."

"Yes, she does."

"Would you have her address?"

"I'm sorry, but I couldn't possibly . . ."

"I understand. A phone number where I can reach her?"

"I'm afraid not. But there may be a listing."

"I'll check. What's her husband's name?"

"Andrew." Odd inflection. As if the name tasted bad in her mouth or stirred up an unpleasantness in her memory.

"And hers?"

"Stacy." Justine hesitated. "Is it important, your reason for wanting to get in touch with Mrs. Vanowen?"

"It could be. A personal matter."

Another pause. Then, "Rubicon Bay."

"Pardon?"

"They live in Rubicon Bay."

"Where would that be?"

"Southwest shore, on the California side."

Cape showed her the photos of the two men, side by side. "Is one of these Andrew Vanowen?"

She pointed to the one of the older, silver-haired man. The oddness was in her expression this time, a darkening that might have been dislike or old anger or maybe both.

"Do you know Vanowen?" he asked.

"No. We've met, but . . . no."

"How about the other man?"

"I've seen him before, but I don't know his name."

"Seen him here at the hotel? Or around the area?"

"Both."

"Another local resident, then."

"I think so, yes." Justine had had enough questions; she said in her by-rote voice, "Now may I show you something for your wife or lady friend?"

"Sorry. I don't have either one."

"Then if you'll excuse me . . ."

He watched her walk away. She had the kind of loose, rolling walk that makes a man wonder what a woman would be like in bed. Horny Cape, ever hungry to make up for all those faithful years. He almost felt ashamed.

* * *

Rubicon Bay.

One of a bunch of little enclaves strung along the lakeshore, along an inlet with the same name. Highway 89 hugged the shoreline here, running in twisty loops through trees and around vast protrusions of granite. Heavily forested slopes came down close on the west: Bliss State Park. There was woodland on the lake side to shield a few score year-round and summer homes. On the south side of the park, he'd passed through a couple of hamlets. None over here, though. Not even a roadside store where he could stop to ask directions.

Cape took the first side road that opened east off the highway. It led him down through pine and fir, past short dead-end lanes and driveways that accessed half-concealed houses. Some of the mailboxes had names on them, but none was Vanowen. He kept driving around, backtracking, until he spotted another car just swinging into one of the driveways. The car stopped at the box there, and the driver, a youngish brunette, got out to pick up her mail. Cape pulled over, put on the salesman's smile as he poked his head out the window.

"Excuse me. I'm looking for the Vanowens, and I seem to have gotten myself lost. It's like a maze in here."

The Corvette as much as the smile put her at ease. In her world, strangers driving beat-up old cars were a threat, but strangers driving expensive sports cars were just plain rich folk. She told him, readily enough, that the Vanowens lived in the last house on Waterwing Drive, right on the lake.

Cape followed her directions, found Waterwing Drive, and drove along it for two hundred yards or so to where it dead-ended at a steep, gated driveway. The gate was open, so he drove on through. Halfway down, the drive jogged, and he could see the house. Big, made of cut pine logs and redwood shakes, thick woods crowding in on both sides. T-shaped pier and a boathouse behind it. A carport on the near side was empty, but an older-model black Mercedes with Nevada plates sat slewed on a pine-needled parking area in front.

He stopped alongside the Mercedes, walked up on a narrow

stoop, and rang the bell. No answer. After a minute he rang it again. Nothing. The third push finally produced results. Footsteps, the rattling of a lock, and the door opened and a woman stood there looking at him.

He'd been measured, dissected, and categorized by any number of less attractive women than this one. Seldom quite as fast or as thoroughly, though. There was a resemblance to the face in the photographs, but she wasn't Stacy Vanowen. Older, thirty or so. Dark-haired, sloe-eyed, wet-lipped. Wearing a one-piece black Spandex bathing suit and a sheer beach wrap. Long legs, narrow hips, smattering of freckles that trailed down into the front of the suit. In one hand was a tall glass of clear, bubbly liquid with ice and lime. The shine in the sloe eyes said she had a lot more gin or vodka tonic inside her.

He rated high enough to win a slow, loose, slightly crooked grin. "Well," she said. "And what're you selling?"

"What makes you think I'm selling something?"

"You have that look. Don't tell me you're not a salesman?"

"I used to be. No more."

"Everybody's a salesman, in one way or another."

"Maybe so," Cape agreed. "I'm looking for Stacy Vanowen."

"Uh-huh. Lots of people do."

"Do what?"

"Look for Stacy. Look *at* her, too. She's a prettier piece than I am, dammit."

"Is she here?"

"Nope. Nobody's here but me."

"When will she be home?"

"Who knows? Whenever she gets here."

"I'd like to talk to her. What's a good time to catch her?"

"If you want to catch Stacy, you'd better be a fast runner. What's your name, salesman?"

"Cape. Matt Cape."

"Short and sweet. I like it."

"I'm glad. What's yours?"

"Lacy."

"Vanowen?"

"God, no. Hammond. Stacy and Lacy. Cute, huh?"

"Sisters?"

"That's us. Stacy and Lacy, Daddy's little joke." All at once her face darkened and she made a spitting mouth. Just as quickly, it cleared and she was grinning again. "He was hilarious, he was. Hilarious old son of a bitch."

Cape said, "You live here?"

"Not me. I'm the poor relation. Little sister lets me come over and play with her toys when there's nobody else around."

"Uh-huh."

"She feels sorry for me. Thinks I'm an alcoholic."

"Are you?"

"You bet. Damn good one, too. Very controlled. I could give lessons."

Cape slid the photos partway out of his pocket. The one of the ice-eyed man was on top. He held that one up.

"Recognize this man?"

Lacy looked, blinked, frowned. "Where'd you get that?"

"I'd rather give your sister the answer to that question."

"Oh, you would."

"If you don't mind."

The dark look and spitting mouth again; and again, as mercurially as before, her mood changed and she burst out laughing. A rich, bawdy laugh that said she was genuinely amused.

"What's funny?" Cape asked her.

"You know who he is?"

"No. Who is he?"

"If you don't know, how come you have his picture?"

"It's a little complicated."

"I'll just bet it is. And you don't want to explain it to anyone but Stacy."

"Or her husband."

"Aha." The laugh rolled out again. "Those other photos in your pocket—little sister?"

"Two of them."

"Pornographic? Let me see."

"Just snapshots. Nobody in them but her."

"Well, that's too bad. Who's in the others?"

"One other. Your sister's husband."

Lacy thought that was even funnier. The laughter rolled and echoed, finally caught in her throat and made her cough. She drowned the rest of her mirth with the last third of her drink.

"I haven't laughed this hard in weeks," she said a little breathlessly. "So it's like that, is it."

"Like what?"

"Come on, what're you selling? And who to?"

"I'm not selling anything."

"Shakedown? That's what they call it, right?"

"Wrong."

"What're you up to, then? Oh, I know. You're a private detective."

"Wrong again. I'm here to do the Vanowens a favor."

"Sure you are. And yourself a bigger one in return."

"Look," Cape said, "I don't really care what you think of me or my motives. If your sister's cheating on her husband, or vice versa, it's none of my concern. That isn't why or how I came into possession of these photos."

Lacy's amusement had vanished. Now she looked sullen, unhappy. "Shit," she said.

"How about telling me the name of the man in this photo?"

"No. Ask Stacy, when you see her. Or Andrew."

"The phone number here? So I can call later."

"It's unlisted."

"I know. I checked the directory before I drove out here."

"Well, you'll just have to drive out here again."

"So you won't let me have the number."

"Salesman, I won't let you have a goddamn thing."

"Will you at least tell your sister I stopped by?"

"Why should I? None of my business. You as much as said so."

"If you change your mind," Cape said, "I'll be at the Lakeside Grand in Stateline. Staying there tonight if I can get a room. In the casino after seven o'clock, either way. If neither of them wants to see me in person, they can call my room or have me paged."

"I've already forgotten you. More important things on my mind."

"Such as?"

"Such as how much gin to put in my next drink."

* * *

Cape stopped the 'Vette at the top of the driveway, next to the Vanowen mailbox. On a piece of scrap paper he wrote a note addressed to both Andrew and Stacy Vanowen—the same information he'd given Lacy, plus his name at the bottom. He put the note in the mailbox.

Twenty-four hours was all he'd give them. If they hadn't made contact by this time tomorrow, he'd be on his way to someplace else. Even good deeds had a patience limit and a time limit.

10

APE looked at the ace of clubs he'd just been dealt, glanced again at his down card: ace of hearts. The dealer had an eight showing. Cape was at the end of the blackjack table to the dealer's left; when his turn came again, he flipped over the diamond ace and laid it alongside the club ace. He said, "Splitting these," and doubled his twenty-five-dollar bet. The dealer slid one card facedown under each of the aces. Cape didn't look at these.

The dealer turned his hole card. Jack to go with the eight. Eighteen. After the house paid the two other players whose hands beat eighteen, Cape let the dealer do the unveiling of his down cards. Deuce to go with the first ace, six to go with the second ace. Another pair of losers.

"Tough luck," one of the other players said. "Just isn't your night, looks like."

Three hundred and sixty in the hole now. Cape said, "Looks like," and raked up his handful of remaining chips. He quit the table, started toward the hotel lobby to see if he had any messages.

He was halfway there, threading his way through the noisy crowd, when somebody fell into step beside him. A hand touched his arm, lightly. When he stopped and swung his head, he was looking into the cold eyes of the olive-skinned man in the photograph.

"Cape, isn't it?" Caviar voice: slick, grainy, salt-oily. "Matthew Cape?"

"That's right."

"Let's go to the casino bar, Mr. Cape. Have a drink and talk."

"Suits me."

The other man stayed close on the walk across to the bar, as if to make sure Cape didn't try to get away. They took an empty table in one corner. Cold Eyes ordered cognac from a waitress in a skimpy purple-and-gold outfit. Cape said he'd have the same.

Once they were alone, he said, "You know my name, but I don't know yours."

"No? I thought you'd have found it out by now. You seem to be pretty resourceful that way."

Cape shrugged. "I figured one of the Vanowens would supply it. Which of them told you about me? Stacy or Andrew? Or was it the sister, Lacy?"

"Does it matter?"

"Not really. I'm just wondering how you found me."

"I've lived in this area a long time. Let's just say I have contacts." He leaned back, crossed his legs. A fat gold ring on one finger caught the neon bar lights, seemed to throw out sparks. An even fatter turquoise-and-silver ring gleamed on his other hand. His lightweight beige suit was shantung silk; the pale blue shirt was silk, too, and the mirror-gloss black shoes looked Italian made. "It's Mahannah, by the way," he said. "Vince Mahannah."

"Mr. Mahannah."

"What would you guess my profession to be?"

"I'm not good at guessing games."

"Give it a try anyway."

"Same business as Andrew Vanowen?"

"Do I look like a venture capitalist? The odds are poor in that kind of business, unless you have an MBA and the right kind of background. Too much risk, too easy to cash out all at once."

"Gambling's also a risky business."

Mahannah cocked an eyebrow. "Is that what you think I am? A gambler?"

"This is a Nevada casino, you seem at home here, and you use terms like 'poor odds' and 'cash out.' Good a guess as any."

"So it is," Mahannah said. "I have a number of interests, as a matter of fact, but I admit gambling is one of them. What about you?"

"Gambling is one of my interests, too."

"Professionally?"

"No. I'm strictly an amateur."

"The high-stakes kind of amateur?"

"Depends on the game."

"Is that why you're in Stateline? To play some kind of high-stakes game?"

"Would you believe me if I said no?"

"Try me."

Their drinks arrived. Mahannah sat warming his between long-fingered, delicate-looking hands. Gambler's hands. Cape nibbled his cognac, set the snifter down.

He said, "I used to be a salesman for a company that manufactures industrial valves in Rockford, Illinois. Dull work. So I decided to retire and do what I've always wanted to do—see some of the country, live it up a little."

"And you finance this new lifestyle how? By gambling?"

"No. I had some money saved."

"A man can always use more, though."

"I'm not looking to get it the way you're thinking."

"What way is that?"

"Look," Cape said, "why don't we quit sparring and get down to it. You've got a notion that I'm here to try some kind of scam with a handful of photographs. The truth is just the opposite. I'm here to warn you and the Vanowens that somebody else might be planning a scam, one that involves the three of you."

Mahannah cocked the eyebrow again. "Who would that somebody be?"

"A couple of small-time grifters I met in San Francisco two days ago. Tanya and Boone Judson—at least, that's what they're calling themselves. Names mean anything to you?"

"No."

"They claim to be brother and sister, but they're either married or shacked up. Cardsharps working the convention circuit. He's the mechanic, and a pretty good one. She does the roping and steering. Marked cards—shaded decks."

Mahannah seemed to be looking at him in a new way. "How'd you meet these two?"

"I got roped into one of their poker cons, spotted the gaff before it was too late."

"And did what about it?"

Cape told him.

Mahannah said, "So you left Frisco with the satchelful of money."

"No. I divvied it up, took my share, and returned the rest to the other players."

"Did you, now. How big was your share?"

"Exact amount of my losses, plus a sixth of two thousand that belonged to the Judsons."

"No more than that?"

"Not a penny more," Cape said.

"Good for you." Mahannah's smile was all mouth; the eyes, unblinking in the half-light, were an almost reptilian black. "This Boone mentioned something about Tahoe and seed money, you said. Is that all he let slip?"

"The woman cut him off before he could take it any further."

"What else was in the satchel besides the money and photos?"

"Nothing."

"Describe the Judsons."

Cape did that, in detail.

"Neither one is familiar," Mahannah said. "If I'd seen them, I'd remember."

"Question is, what kind of scam could they be planning with you and the Vanowens?"

"Same kind you caught them doing, maybe. I host a private poker game once a month at my home. Friends, mostly—Andy Vanowen's one. Now and then, when we can't round up enough players, we let a stranger sit in."

"High stakes?"

"It can be that kind of game, yes."

"Next one coming up soon?"

"Saturday night. These grifters might've gotten wind of it somehow, figured to worm the Boone character into the game. But he couldn't've pulled off a shade-work gimmick with us. No way anybody brings his own decks into my game." The mouth-stretch, the reptilian stare. "No way anybody cheats in my game, ever, if he knows what's good for him. He'd have to be a damn fool to even try."

"Does Mrs. Vanowen sit in?"

"Stacy? Hell, no. Down-and-dirty poker's not her style."

"A lady," Cape said.

"That's right. A lady."

"So why did the Judsons have the photos of her? Where does she fit into a poker con?"

"She couldn't fit in. No way."

"Could be she knows the Judsons from somewhere. Or they know her."

"The last people she'd be likely to rub elbows with are short-con artists," Mahannah said. "But I'll ask her. You have those photos on you?"

Cape laid them on the table, watched Mahannah study each one in turn. Nothing showed in his face; the cold eyes still didn't blink.

"The studio portraits of you and Vanowen," Cape said. "How would the Judsons have gotten hold of them?"

Mahannah thought about it. Shook his head and said, "I don't know." He put away some of his cognac. "I'd like to keep these."

"The one of you, sure. I'd prefer to deliver the others to the Vanowens personally."

"Why? You don't trust me to do it? Tell them what you told me?"

"That's not it. I like to finish what I start."

"If you're thinking of some kind of reward—"

"Money's not an issue. I wouldn't take it if it was offered."

"A man with scruples, to a fault," Mahannah said. "You interest me, Cape. I don't run across many selfless men."

Cape said, "I used to be selfish as hell. I figure it's time to find out how the other type lives."

Mahannah's chuckle was almost genuine. "Suppose Andy and Stacy don't want to see you."

"That's up to them. I'll be here one more day. If I don't connect with either of them, I'll leave the photos in an envelope at the desk with your name on it."

"Fair enough." Mahannah finished his cognac, fished a couple of bills out of his pocket, tossed them on the table. He stood up. "If you're all you seem to be, I owe you a favor, and so do the Vanowens."

"Forget it. I won't be around long enough to collect."

When Mahannah was gone, Cape looked at the bills on the table. A twenty and a ten. Whatever else he might be, Vince Mahannah was no piker.

11

THE phone was ringing when Cape stepped out of the shower. He swung a towel around himself, went out dripping to cut off the noise.

"Mr. Cape?" Woman's voice, low-pitched, tentative.

"Yes?"

"This is Stacy Vanowen. I understand you want to speak to my husband and me about some photographs."

"I didn't mention the photographs in my note."

She said coolly, "Vince Mahannah is a good friend of ours."

"So I understand."

"I . . . don't know those people you met in San Francisco. Andrew says he doesn't, either."

"Let's hope you never have anything to do with them."

"Yes." Pause. "We'll be lunching at the Lakepoint Country Club today. Andrew asked me to invite you to join us."

"A brief meeting is all that's necessary—"

"He insists. The Lakepoint is in Stateline, not far from your hotel. At the end of Lakepoint Drive."

"I'll find it."

"Twelve-thirty. The reservation is in his name."

* * *

The breakfast buffet was crowded, a line of people waiting for seats. Cape paused, glancing around. He hated standing in lines, even short ones. Skip breakfast? He wasn't hungry, but he could use some coffee.

His gaze caught and held the occupant of one of the two-person booths in the middle of the room. The Eurasian woman from Milady's Pleasure. In her purple-and-gold outfit, eating alone.

He walked over to her, bypassing the hostess. "Good morning. Justine, isn't it?"

"Yes? Oh . . . the man with the photographs."

"Cape, Matt Cape. Would you mind if I joined you?"

"Well . . ."

"No other available seats. And the line over there is getting longer."

The striking almond-shaped eyes studied him. "I won't be here much longer, so I guess it'll be all right."

He sat. The table was small and mostly covered with her breakfast—scrambled eggs, bacon, hotcakes, orange juice, coffee.

"You must be hungry," he said.

"Well, free breakfast is one of the perks of my job."

"Nice perk."

"It's a good job. Did you find Mrs. Vanowen?"

"Yes. I'm having lunch with her and her husband today."

Smile, shrug. She reached out for her orange juice. Light glinted off the bracelet on her wrist: patterned silver, with a heart-shaped clasp.

Cape said to the waitress who had just come up, "Just coffee, thanks." Then, to Justine, "What're the Vanowens like?"

"You don't know?"

"Nothing much about either of them."

"I only know Mrs. Vanowen as a customer," Justine said carefully. "She doesn't say much, but she seems nice."

"She have a job or profession?"

"Not that I know of."

"How about her husband?"

Justine's gaze flicked away, flicked back. "What about him?"

"I understand he's a venture capitalist."

"Oh . . . yes. Very successful, very high-powered."

"You don't like him, do you?"

"What makes you say that?"

"The look on your face yesterday when I showed you his photo. The look on your face right now."

"I really don't know the man."

"Or want to?"

"Or want to. He's too . . . aggressive."

"Man who won't take no for an answer?"

"That type, yes."

"If I'm not getting too personal, you make him take no from you?"

Her gaze slid away again.

"Don't answer the question if you'd rather not."

"I don't date married men," she said, "no matter how insistent they are or how much money and power they have."

"That's a good philosophy."

"It almost cost me my job."

"You mean he did. The vindictive type, too."

"That's all past. I don't care to dredge it up again."

"I won't ask you to," Cape said. Then, "I like your bracelet."

Her smile came back. "It is nice, isn't it? My son gave it to me for my birthday. He's only fifteen, but he has really good taste."

"Fifteen? You don't seem old enough to have a son that age."

"Thank you. I was nineteen when I married his father."

"Not still married, I take it?"

"Divorced eight years ago, before Gary and I moved up here from Sacramento."

"Separated after twelve years," Cape said, "divorce pending. My fault, not hers."

"In my case, we were both at fault."

"Any other children?"

"No, just Gary." She stroked the bracelet with the tip of her finger. "He's the best. You know, he bought this with his own money. He works part-time as a caddy at the country club."

"Lakepoint Country Club?"

"That's right. How did you know?"

"Just a guess. It's where I'm having lunch with the Vanowens."

"Oh. Well, you'll like the restaurant. I've eaten there a few times with Gary and my roommate."

"Roommate?"

"Her name is Lilith. She also works at Lakepoint, in their payroll department. We share expenses—wages aren't high in this area, at least not for single mothers and widows."

Cape's coffee arrived. The waitress said to Justine, "Will there be anything else, Ms. Coolidge?" in chilly tones.

"No, nothing, Ms. Adams." Just as chilly.

"Why the freeze?" Cape asked when they were alone again. "You and the waitress."

"We had a problem a while back," Justine said. "She thought I was competition for a man she was dating."

"And she was wrong?"

"Completely. I don't play that sort of game either."

"Are you in a relationship now?"

". . . No."

"Neither am I. Will you have dinner with me tonight?"

"I thought that's what you were leading up to. I'm flattered, Mr. Cape—"

"Matt."

"I'm flattered, but we're not supposed to date guests. House rule."

"Rules were made to be broken."

"Not the Lakeside Grand's, and not mine."

"Suppose I weren't staying here?"

"But you are staying here."

"I could check out, move someplace else."

Raised eyebrow. "Would you really do that?"

"I think I might."

"The answer is still no." She softened the words with another of her smiles. "You seem like a nice guy, but I'm not in the market for a fling, and there's something about you that says you're not in the market for anything else."

"True enough," he admitted.

"I really am sorry."

"So am I." Cape finished his coffee, stood up. "The best to you and your son, Justine. I mean that."

"Thank you. And to you, Matt Cape."

Win some, lose some. And just as well to be a loser this time. Justine deserved better than men like him and Andrew Vanowen and the ex-husband who'd let her get away. The kind of man she deserved was an older version of the kid who'd saved his money to buy her a patterned silver bracelet for her birthday.

12

H E spent the rest of the morning making the rounds of the other casinos. In Harrah's he won a hundred and fifty playing black-jack. In Caesar's, another ninety. One of the craps layouts was getting some play in the Harvey's; the shooter, a sweating bald man in his sixties, was riding a hot streak and betting heavily. Cape watched him make another pass, moved in, and put fifty on the pass line. Eleven, another winner. He let his winnings ride. The next roll was an eight. Cape put another twenty on the Come line, and the shooter made his eight point the hard way, with a pair of fours, on the third roll. The bald man paused to wipe his streaming face; his eyes had a glazed look. Subtle change in the vibes. Cape switched half his stack of chips to Don't Pass. Right choice: The next roll was boxcars. Craps for the shooter, another winner for Cape.

All right. No luck with Justine, but a nice little run of luck on the gambling end; he was close to five hundred ahead for his twenty-some hours in Stateline. Hang for a while, try to ride it up? Or put it on hold and move on when he was done with the Vanowens?

The red message light on his room phone was blinking. Voice-mail message from Vince Mahannah: Call him back any time, he expected to be home all day.

Cape tapped out the number. Mahannah said without preamble, "How would you like to sit in on my poker game tomorrow night?"

"I was thinking I might get back on the road this afternoon."

"Someplace you need to be?"

"No."

"Then stick around a couple of days. Play some poker, leave Sunday."

"Tell me something. Why the invitation?"

"Would you buy it if I said it was the favor I mentioned last night?"

Cape said, "It wouldn't be a favor if I lost money."

"No, it wouldn't. Truth is, we're shorthanded. Just five of us this time, and I don't like playing with less than six."

"I can't afford to get into a high-stakes game."

"You won't be," Mahannah said. "Not all of mine are like that. No high rollers in this one, just friends of mine. How much can you afford to lose?"

Cape thought about it. "A few thousand, maybe. But not for an hour or two's entertainment."

"You don't strike me as the wild-hair type. That kind of play is the only way you'd lose a few thousand in an hour or two. Table stakes, twenty-dollar ante, no limit on the bets, four-limit on the raises. Straight poker, nothing fancy."

"I don't know," Cape said. "I had a good run in the casinos this morning, and I'm not sure I want to push my luck."

"Sometimes pushing it means riding it."

"Sometimes."

"Think it over. Give me another call if you're interested."

"I'll do that. Thanks for the invitation."

"Don't thank me unless you play and win."

Lakepoint Country Club.

Big, precision-landscaped place on the lakeshore. Most of the eighteen-hole golf course spread over a jut of land flanked by thick stands of trees—chlorophyll-bright greens, manmade lagoon, rolling fairways, not too many hazards. Clubhouse and restaurant and outbuildings made of pine and some darker wood, embellished with native stone and plenty of glass. Playpen for the rich. The greens fees would be high, membership fee upwards of five thousand a year: Keep out the riffraff.

Cape had played a couple of courses like this one in the Chicago area. Golf had been part of his salesman's persona, a comfortable, outdoors way to schmooze Emerson's clients and prospective clients. He'd never been very good at the game. Nor developed the passion for it some people did. It had been a means to an end, a take-it-or-leave-it pastime that he didn't miss at all. The new Cape, standing here looking out over all that green opulence, was as alien to golf as the old Cape would have been to the bunch of skydivers in Phoenix.

He parked in a large lot, went up onto the path that separated the lot from the woodsy grounds and led around to the clubhouse. When he passed a screen of oleanders, a section of lawn opened up and let him see another path bordering one of the fairways. A gardener's cart stood there, two people talking beside it. The dark, pudgy man in uniform was probably one of the grounds crew; the tall woman in white blouse and shorts was Lacy Hammond.

She was facing Cape's way, recognized him. She broke off her conversation with the gardener and cut across the lawn in long, loose strides to intercept Cape before he reached the clubhouse.

"Hello, salesman," she said. Sober this morning, and apparently none the worse for yesterday's drinking. "You do get around."

"I might say the same for you."

"I live in this area. You don't."

"Play golf, do you?"

"When the mood strikes. I'm pretty good, too. Been whacking balls since I was twelve."

"I'll bet you have."

She let him hear her bawdy laugh. "You don't look much like a ball-whacker yourself."

"I used to be. Not anymore."

"So what're you doing here? No, wait, let me guess. Baby sister?"

"And her husband. I've been invited to lunch."

"My, my. You really must be some salesman."

"I told you yesterday," Cape said, "I'm not selling anything."

"Then how come the free lunch?"

"It won't be free. I'll pay for my own."

"Andy won't like that. He enjoys throwing his money around. Sometimes he even throws some my way."

"And you don't duck when he does."

"I don't drop it, either. Lacy plays catch with both hands."

"Uh-huh."

"Money and men both," she said. Her voice was bantering, but her gaze was analytical. "Two hands, squeeze hard, hang on tight."

"And use 'em up fast, money and men both."

"Why not? The using up works both ways."

"Pretty cynical attitude."

"You could benefit from it. If you played your cards right."

Cape said, "I won't be in Tahoe long enough," and started away.

She called after him, "You give up easy, salesman."

"That's the way I do everything these days," he said without turning. "Easy."

13

ANDREW Vanowen said, "You're not what I expected, Cape."

"No? What did you expect?"

"Older man, glib, not so low-key."

"Should I take that as a compliment?"

"He didn't mean it that way," Stacy Vanowen said.

"Stacy." Sharp, but without looking at her. As if he were telling a pet to be quiet.

She smiled faintly, looked out through the tall window on her right. A slant of sunshine lay across that side of her face, along her bare shoulder and arm. On the lake, on the glass, the sunlight glittered hotly. On her it seemed cooler, a paler shade, like light rays on sculptured white marble. Reach over and touch her, and she'd have a marble feel—cool, smooth, surface-soft. The type of woman who would never sweat, even when she was making love. Direct opposite of her sister.

Of her husband, too. He was like something made out of bone and tightly strung wire, covered with tanned rawhide and powered by a generator tuned so high you could hear it hum and crackle. He attacked his crab cocktail as if it were an enemy. The crab cocktails had been waiting along with the Vanowens when Cape was shown to their table in the packed, beam-ceilinged restaurant.

One for him as well. Ordered in advance. He hadn't touched it. And wouldn't.

Through a red mouthful, Vanowen asked, "What is it you do, exactly?"

"Do?" Cape said.

"Your livelihood. What's your business?"

"You might say I'm retired."

"From what?"

"The rat race."

"That's an evasion."

"Not really. I used to work for a manufacturing firm in Illinois, and I got fed up with the grind."

"And now you collect photographs of people you don't know and travel around selling them, is that it?"

"No, that's not it. Everybody seems to think I'm a salesman. That's what I used to be. It's not what I am today."

"Everybody's a salesman."

"Not me. Not anymore."

"Perhaps Mr. Cape is simply a good Samaritan," Stacy Vanowen said. "They do exist, you know."

"Not in my experience." Vanowen finished his cocktail, shoved his plate aside, scrubbed at his mouth with his napkin, looked at his watch, rotated an expensive ring on his left hand—platinum, with a circle of fat diamonds—gestured to the waiter, and said as if there'd been no pause, "Everybody has motives. Everybody's got an agenda."

"Not me," Cape said again.

Stacy Vanowen said, "I'd like to see the photos, Mr. Cape."

He handed her the glossies. Before she could separate them, her husband snatched them out of her hand. He glanced at the two of her, scowled at the one of himself. "This is the studio portrait I had taken for the *BusinessWeek* article last year. What the devil?"

"Let me look at them, Andy."

He allowed her to reclaim the photos. "How could somebody get hold of that one? Magazine didn't use it after all, some kind of space problem, and they sent it back. I don't remember what I did with it." He asked her, "Do you?"

"You said you were going to burn it."

"I thought I did." Vanowen rotated the fancy ring again, his eyes still on Cape. "I take lousy photographs. Thought this one was all right at first, but I'm glad *BusinessWeek* didn't use it. Makes me look stiff, like I've got a broom handle stuck up my ass."

Cape said, "Maybe this copy came from the photographer."

"I doubt it. He's a friend of mine, he wouldn't sell or give away any copies without my permission."

"Did you give out any to friends or business associates?"

"No. My secretary might have, but she usually mentions that sort of request. I'll ask her about it."

"I don't like this," Stacy Vanowen said. "These pictures of me . . ."

Cape asked her, "Can you tell when they were taken?"

"It had to've been recently, within the past month or so. I've only owned this beige outfit a few weeks." She hugged her arms. "They make me feel cold. As if I've been . . . violated."

"Damn right it's a violation," Vanowen said. "These people you told Vince Mahannah about, Cape, the ones in San Francisco—"

"Boone and Tanya Judson."

"Grifters, cardsharps." He made an angry gesture, shifted in his chair, leaned back, leaned forward. "Why did they have these photos? What's their game?"

"I don't have any answers for you, Mr. Vanowen."

"The poker scam idea doesn't make sense. My wife isn't a player, she never gambles at all. She—"

He broke off as more food arrived. Three orders: one seafood salad, two plates of some kind of fileted whitefish. Cape glanced at his fish and then ignored it.

Stacy Vanowen said, "What if it's some kind of kidnapping scheme?"

Her husband jumped as if she'd goosed him. "Kidnapping?"

"It's possible, Andrew. We're well off, aren't we?"

"They wouldn't need seed money for something like that," Cape said.

"That might've been just a lie to mislead you."

"There's also the photo of Vince Mahannah. Why include him if you and your husband are kidnapping targets?"

"God, I don't know. Who knows how people like that think?"

"It's a big jump from convention-circuit con games to a capital offense. I don't see those two making it."

Vanowen said, "You're no expert, Cape."

"You're right, I'm not."

"All right, then. We don't know what they're up to, that's the bottom line." Vanowen poked at his filet, banged the fork down without eating, pinched the ridge of muscle along his lower lip instead. "Mahannah passed on their description, but I want to hear it from you. In detail."

Cape obliged.

"Total strangers," Vanowen said. "Stacy?"

"Yes. To me, too."

"Well, if either of them shows up around here, they'll damn well be sorry—"

His shirt pocket buzzed. Cell phone. He had it out and switched on and jammed against his ear in three fast movements. He said, "Vanowen," listened, said, "How much?" and listened again. Then he said, "Twenty minutes," and made the cell disappear as swiftly as he'd produced it.

His wife said, "You're leaving, I suppose."

"Have to. Business. You go ahead and finish your lunch."

"I'm not hungry."

"Eat it anyway." Vanowen snaked a hand inside the pocket of his sand-colored slacks, brought it out clutching a checkbook. Inside was a loose check, already made out. He dropped it on the table, used one finger to slide it over toward Cape.

Cape ignored it, just as he'd ignored the crab cocktail and the fileted whitefish.

"Go ahead," Vanowen said, "take it."

"No, thanks."

"It's for two hundred and fifty dollars."

"I wouldn't care if it was twenty-five hundred or twenty-five thousand. I don't want your money."

"Why the hell not?"

"Because I didn't earn it. Because I don't take money for offering a helping hand. Because I spent most of my life letting myself be bought in one way or another. Because I'm tired of everybody I've met the past two days misjudging me and my motives. Take your pick."

Vanowen stared at him as if he were a new and baffling species. Abruptly he got to his feet. He said to Cape, "Suit yourself," said to his wife, "I don't know what time I'll be home," and power-walked his way out of the restaurant.

Cape picked up the check, tore it into small pieces, and dropped the pieces onto his plate. He said, "Classic type A, your husband. He'll have a massive coronary someday, if he doesn't slow down."

"I've told him the same thing. He won't listen." She sighed, pushed her salad around on the plate. "He can be overbearing and abrasive, and he thinks money is God and he's one of its disciples. But he's a decent man underneath. Really, he is."

Cape doubted that. Andrew Vanowen, as far as he was concerned, was just what Justine had led him to believe—an arrogant, high-powered asshole. Stacy Vanowen knew it, too, despite what she'd said. The knowledge was in her eyes, in the tight line of her mouth.

He said, "I'll take your word for it."

After a time she said, "Those people, the Judsons or whoever they are . . ."

"What about them?"

"*Do* we have anything to fear from them? Your honest opinion."

"I doubt it. Whatever their game was, it's likely I sidetracked it when I took their cash and got hold of those photographs. And I'd be willing to bet it was nothing as heavy as a kidnapping."

"That's reassuring. Anyway, it's our problem now. You'll be leaving Tahoe soon, I suppose."

"Soon enough. Your friend Mahannah invited me to sit in on his poker game tomorrow night."

"Oh? Are you going to?"

"Haven't made up my mind yet."

Pick, pick at the salad. "When you do leave, where will you go?"

"Reno, maybe. North from there or east into Utah. Depends on my mood at the time."

"I envy you," she said. "Sometimes I wish I could just get in my car and drive and keep on driving."

"Why don't you?"

"I'm a woman, for one thing. Women alone are targets."

"Not if they're careful."

"You can't be careful twenty-four/seven, can you?"

"You have a point. Nobody can."

"Besides, I'm married and I love my husband and most of the time I'm reasonably content with my life. I leave the free-and-easy lifestyle to my sister."

"Lacy?"

"How do you know her name?"

"I met her. Yesterday, at your house. She didn't tell you?"

"No, she didn't."

"I'm not surprised. I gathered you're not close."

"I wish we were. What did she say about me?"

"Nothing worth repeating."

"I can imagine." Pause. "I suppose she . . . came on to you?"

"Not exactly. Why, does she come on to most men she meets?'

"More often than not." Disapproval in her tone, and a hint of malice in what she said next. "My sister never met a penis she didn't like."

Cape's laugh put a tint of color in her cheeks.

"That probably sounds prudish," she said. "But the truth is, I'm just a little jealous. Lacy has always done exactly what she wants and I've always been the good girl, the practical one."

"I'd say she's a little jealous of you, too."

"Not of who I am. Of what I have. She— Oh, God, why am I talking like this? I don't know you and you don't really care about my family situation."

Cape said nothing.

"You're not eating," Stacy Vanowen said. "Aren't you hungry?"

"I like to make my own choices from a menu."

"Oh, I see. Another of my husband's less than endearing traits. He thinks he knows what's best for everybody."

"I've stopped letting other people make my decisions for me," Cape said, "even the small ones. Pretty liberating."

"I wish I could do the same."

"One of these days, maybe you will."

"Yes," she said, "maybe," but she didn't sound as if she believed it.

A piece of paper was tucked under one of the Corvette's windshield wipers. Note written in purple ink and a bold scrawl: *Easy*

does it, salesman. 246 Lake Summit Road, Cave Rock. Any time af-
ter 7 o'clock. The signature was the single letter *L*.

Cape smiled faintly, folded the note, and put it in his shirt
pocket. Two reasons to stay, now. Vince Mahannah's poker game
tomorrow night, tonight an attractive woman who had never met a
penis she didn't like.

Why not?

14

CAPE returned to the clubhouse, found a public phone, and called Vince Mahannah. He said, "I've decided to take you up on your invitation."

"Good. I was hoping you would."

"What time?"

"We usually start around nine."

"Suits me."

Mahannah gave him an address in Glenbrook, on the Nevada shore, and directions; Cape wrote them down. "Get here earlier if you want something to eat. Plenty of food, drinks."

"I'll keep that in mind."

"The other matter," Mahannah said. "You had lunch with the Vanowens? Gave them the photographs?"

"Yes."

"Their reaction?"

"Angry wait-and-see on his part."

"That's Andy. And Stacy?"

"Worried. She brought up the subject of kidnapping."

"What? I don't see it that way."

"Neither do I."

"Andy reassure her?"

"No. He had other business on his mind. I did what I could after he left."

"You spent time with Stacy alone?'

"A few minutes."

"What do you think of her?"

"Attractive," Cape said, "and unhappy."

"Why do you say that?"

"General impression. And some things she said."

"About what?"

"Her marriage, for one."

"You asked her about her marriage?" Edge in Mahannah's voice now. "Her private life?"

"I didn't ask. She volunteered."

"What, specifically?"

"Nothing, specifically."

"You wouldn't be planning to see her again, would you?"

"No reason to."

"Then don't. Any problems she might have are none of your business. You understand?"

That edge—protectiveness, the kind that went beyond simple friendship. Possession or unsated hunger, one or the other.

"I understand," Cape said.

Time on his hands. The rest of the day until seven o'clock. He took the Corvette east on Highway 50, up into the mountains, then down a steep grade into Carson City.

Not much to interest him there. Silver-domed capital building, state museums, a few casinos. Small-town feel. He drove on to SR 341, turned off and wound up into the hills to Virginia City.

More to his liking. Home of the Comstock Lode, the silver strike that had helped build San Francisco and finance the Union Army during the Civil War. Lots of old buildings restored to give the place a nineteenth-century boomtown ambience. Touristy, but not too bad. He wandered the hillside streets, drank a beer in the Bucket of Blood Saloon, let an old-fashioned one-armed bandit steal a few dollars in another saloon, took a tour of Piper's Opera House, where Edwin Booth and Lotta Crabtree had performed in Virginia City's heyday.

On one of the upper streets was a brick church, St. Mary's in the Mountains. He went in and sat for a time in the cool emptiness. First church he'd been in since St. Vincent's in Rockford. No reason for staying there as long as he did; no amazing grace to save a wretch like him. Just that he liked the atmosphere—history mixed with piety. Another good, quiet place to sit and think.

It was after five when he got back to Stateline and the Lakeside Grand. Upstairs, he keyed open the door to his room, took a step inside. And stopped, staring.

The room wasn't the same as he'd left it. Drawers pulled out, bedclothes ripped off, mattress yanked askew, his suitcase open and empty on the floor. And sitting in the larger of the two armchairs, the person responsible for all the upheaval.

Tanya Judson.

With another little automatic in her hand.

15

SHE popped to her feet as Cape came all the way inside and shut the door. One good look at her, and he knew she was a different woman than the one he'd dealt with in San Francisco. The cool self-possession was gone, for one thing. Sloppy clothes, for another: loose-fitting blouse, chinos, flat shoes. Blond hair tangled, windblown. Purplish welt on one temple. Face set in grim lines, something more than anger and determination in her eyes. Fear. Strong dose of it.

He said, "How'd you know where to find me?"

"Never mind that."

"Okay, then how'd you get in here? Bribe a maid? Tell some half-wit bellboy you're my wife and you forgot your key?"

The gun was steady in her hand, a little purse-size job like the one he'd taken from her in the Conover Arms. "It's not here," she said. She made a menacing gesture with the automatic. "Where is it?"

"Where's what?"

"The money, damn you. The sixteen thousand you stole from us."

"I don't have it anymore."

"Don't fuck with me, Cape. I want that money!"

"I gave it back to the other marks in the game, like I said I would. All except what belonged to me."

"Bullshit."

"God's honest truth. The next morning, before I left the city."

"Two thousand of it was ours!"

"Forfeit charge," Cape said. "I divvied it up six ways."

She made a noise like a cat's hiss. "Your wallet. Toss it on the bed."

"I'm only carrying about two hundred."

"On the bed. Now."

Cape shrugged, flipped his wallet onto the mattress. Tanya leaned over to fumble for it without taking her eyes off him. When she had the thin sheaf of bills out, she held them up in a fan.

"I told you," he said. "Two hundred, give or take."

"Where's the rest of it? You've got more than this."

"I might've lost it all in the casinos."

"Don't give me that crap. Where is it?"

"All right. There's a little under five thousand in the hotel safe."

"Four thousand. What about the other twelve?"

"I told you. Back to the rightful owners."

"I want that money!"

"*You* want it. What about Boone?"

"Screw him. He's a damn fool."

"Is that right?"

"In way over his head. . . . I told him but he wouldn't listen."

"In over his head in what?"

"He can rot in hell for all I care. Him and Rollo both."

"Who's Rollo?"

Headshake.

Cape said, "You walked out on Boone, is that it?"

"Soon as you give me the money, then I'm gone."

"Where is he? Here in Tahoe?"

"Never mind where he is."

"What're Boone and Rollo up to?"

"You think I'm going to tell you?"

"Why not, if you're through with Boone and getting out? What kind of con are they setting up for the Vanowens and Vince Mahannah?"

"How did you—"

"The photographs were in the satchel with the money. Or didn't Boone tell you that?"

"Is that why *you're* here? Those damn photographs?"

"The con, Tanya. Poker scam or something else?"

"Uh-uh. You're not getting anything out of me."

"At least tell me why you're quitting Boone. What happened? He start knocking you around?"

"He'll never lay another hand on me, that's for sure."

"What's got you so scared, Tanya?"

"Scared? What makes you think I'm scared?"

"Your eyes, your voice. That gun in your hand."

"Well, you're wrong. I want out, that's all."

"Out of what?"

"That's enough!" The automatic jabbed, jumped. On her forehead now, little buttons of sweat. "The rest of the money must be in the hotel safe," she said. "Sure, that's it. The whole sixteen thousand."

"Wrong. Just under five thousand, all of it mine."

"We're going down there," she said. "You and me, right now."

"Wrong again. I'm not going anywhere with you."

"I'll use this gun, Cape. I mean it. I'll blow your cock right out of the saddle."

"Tough talk. What good would that do you?"

"I want that money!"

Broken record. Cape walked over to the other chair, sat down: slowly, deliberately.

The hissing cat sound again. "Get up! We're going downstairs."

"No, we're not."

"I'll kill you! You think I won't?"

"I think you won't."

The gun's muzzle danced sideways, and she fired.

Noise halfway between a bang and a pop. The bullet chewed into the carpet alongside Cape's chair. He didn't move, his gaze locked with hers.

"Not even close," he said. "And not very smart. If anybody heard that, they're on the phone right now. It won't take hotel security more than two or three minutes to get up here."

"You son of a bitch!"

"Better get out while you can, Tanya. Only other option you've got is to blow my cock out of the saddle—murder or attempted murder."

Four or five tense seconds.

Then she broke and ran, trailing obscenities.

As soon as the door banged shut after her, Cape was out of the chair and across the room. He eased the door open a crack to listen. No voices, no neighbors alerted by the shot. The bank of elevators was just down the hall; he heard one of the cars whining upward, heard the doors thrum open and then close again.

He ran for the elevators as the car began its descent. Jabbed the down button, kept jabbing it. Fast elevators in the Lakeside Grand: another car was there in less than thirty seconds. It went down fast, too—no stops. When the doors whispered open, he was out in a rush to where he had a full view of the lobby.

She was still in sight, walking fast toward the side entrance, not looking back.

Cape followed her at an oblique angle until she passed through the doors. Then he made a straight run, got outside in time to spot her heading into the parking lot at the rear. All right. That was where he'd left the Corvette, lucking into a space in one of the near rows. Her wheels were somewhere farther back; she was hurrying deeper into the lot on a long diagonal.

He had the 'Vette clear of the parking space and idling near the only exit when she drove past. Clear look at her in profile: She was one of those forward hunchers, both hands tight on the wheel, eyes locked straight ahead. She seemed to have no idea he was there.

Cape let her get clear of the lot before he swung out behind her. She took the loop back down to Lake Tahoe Boulevard, turned west at the light. Her car was a new, pale blue Mitsubishi, California plates and a Hertz rental sticker on the rear bumper—easy enough to keep in sight. She stayed in the left lane, moving in fast spurts, then slowing down. Nervous driving, not the evasive kind. He stayed in the right lane a few car lengths behind.

Back across the line into South Lake Tahoe. Traffic was heavy along motel row: stop and go, stop and go. It wasn't long before she slowed to a crawl, still in the left lane, bunching up cars behind her, the way some drivers do when they're looking for an unfamiliar street or landmark. Going to make a turn pretty soon. Cape squeezed over into her lane.

At the next intersection she veered into the left-turn lane. So did the car behind her, so did Cape. He checked the street sign: Pioneer Trail. She went into Pioneer at a good clip when the light changed, but the woman driving the car in front of Cape was the poky type. He moved up close to try to hurry her or prod her into pulling over. All it did was cause her to slow down even more. Tanya's lead was two hundred yards and growing before they'd gone a fifth of a mile past rustic motels, small apartment complexes, lower middle-class homes on wooded lots.

When the road began to curve, Cape lost sight of the Mitsubishi for short periods. The woman in front of him kept right on poking. The gap was upward of three hundred yards when Tanya disappeared beyond another curve; and when he came around to where he could see some distance ahead, she wasn't on Pioneer any longer. Must've turned off at the next intersection. But which way?

Cape was close on the poky woman's bumper as they approached the intersection. Look left, look right—no sign of the Mitsubishi in either direction. The street to the left was a two-block uphill dead end; he swung off to the right, past a sign that said Black Bart Road. Private houses on small tree-choked lots. Cars parked, cars moving, none of them the Mitsubishi. A few people out and about, none of them Tanya.

He drove around half a dozen blocks, came back and crossed Pioneer Trail, and went up the dead-end street on the other side. No sign of Tanya or the rental car up there, either.

Lost her.

Yeah, or maybe she'd been wise all along—maybe she'd lost him.

16

CAVE Rock was a small hillside settlement on Highway 50 on the Nevada shore. Private homes perched along steep, narrow streets, some new and expensive with expensive views, others older, smaller, less affluent. Two-forty-six Lake Summit Road was one of the latter, a sprawling, boxy pile painted the color of dog vomit, with an oblique view of the lake and not much land around it on any side.

Lacy Hammond opened the door immediately to his ring, as if she'd been standing there on the other side waiting for him. Appraising look, lazy smile. "What, no flowers, no candy? No bottle of expensive liquor?"

"You expect a present?"

"Hell, no. Matter of fact, I wasn't sure you'd show up at all."

"Odds for or against?"

"Even money. What're you looking at, salesman?"

"You, the way you're dressed." Mauve slacks, a sleeveless tank top. Nothing on her feet. No makeup, and her hair carelessly finger-brushed.

"What'd you expect? Slinky gown? Sheer negligee? Bare-ass naked?"

"None of the above."

"Uh-huh. I may be easy, but I'm not trite. Come on in."

Homey disarray—Anna's phrase to describe inoffensively sloppy housekeeping. Mismatched furniture, and no more color sense inside than out. Plaid couch, saffron-hued corduroy chairs, cobalt blue carpet, one wall painted gold with sparkly stuff mixed in.

"Nice place," Cape lied.

"It sucks, and we both know it. Funk junk."

"Why live here if you don't like it?"

"It's mine, that's why. Part of my divorce settlement. My ex got to move upscale—Vegas and a job as an assistant manager of a brand-new casino. I got to stay here and fend for myself."

"Fend for yourself how?"

"You mean what do I do for a living?"

"If it's not a secret."

"It's not. Sponge off men when I can find one who's got money. Sponge off my baby sister and her rich husband. Work as a cocktail waitress in a pinch. I get by."

"I'll bet you do."

"So. What're you drinking, salesman? I'm having Scotch tonight."

"I'll join you. Neat, if it's single malt."

"It's not."

"Over ice, then. Can I use your phone?"

"As long as you don't call somebody long distance."

"Your sister and her husband. If you'll give me the number."

Frown. "What do you want to call them for?"

"Something important to tell them."

"Such as?"

"Listen to my end of the conversation."

"Balls," she said, but she gave him the number.

Four rings, and an answering machine kicked in. Everybody was out tonight; he'd gotten Vince Mahannah's machine when he called there earlier. Cape identified himself, gave the Vanowens the same message he'd given Mahannah: "Tanya Judson is here in Tahoe. Her partner, too, probably. Scared enough to show up at my room at the Grand, waving another gun and demanding the money I took from them in San Francisco. Wouldn't say how she found out where I was staying. Wouldn't give me any idea of what she and Boone are up to, just said he was in over his head with somebody named Rollo and she was walking out on him. I bluffed her into leaving, managed to follow her over into South Lake Tahoe. She's driving a blue Mitsubishi with a Hertz rental sticker. I lost her on Black Bart Road, off Pioneer Trail. She may or may not be staying somewhere in the area—I couldn't tell if she spotted me or not. My suggestion is that you notify the police about her. She seemed pretty desperate. I'll corroborate, if that's what you and Vince Mahannah decide to do."

He broke the connection. When he turned, Lacy said, "For Christ's sake. What was that all about?"

"You haven't talked to your sister today?"

"No. Some woman threatened you with a gun?"

"Let's get that Scotch, and I'll tell you about it."

Lacy said drowsily, "I'm glad you're not one of those clinical types."

"Clinical?"

"Want to talk about it afterward. Tell each other how great it was."

"I don't see any point in verbal replays."

"Neither do I. If sex is any good, it's private when you're done. Words just spoil it." She yawned, stretched. "You married, salesman?"

"Once. Not anymore."

"How long'd it last?"

"Twelve years."

"My first mistake didn't last twelve months. Or even six."

"That's too bad."

"I was nineteen," she said. "His idea of fun was shitkicker bars, dirt bikes, and fifteen-second fucks. No kidding, fifteen seconds every time. You could set your watch by it. Wham, bam, thank you ma'am. Joe the Rabbit."

Cape was silent.

"Number two wasn't much better. Better in the sack, but he liked it rough and kinky. At least he made decent money—I stuck him good for the two years of sadomasochistic bullshit I put up with."

He let that pass, too.

After a time Lacy leaned up on one elbow, gazed down into his face. "I keep thinking about what you told me," she said, serious now. "The photographs, the woman with the gun, all the rest. You don't have any idea what it's all about?"

"None."

"She didn't give you a hint?"

"All she said was what I told you. Boone's in over his head with somebody named Rollo, and she wants out."

"Rollo. Real name or a nickname, I wonder."

"Could be either one."

"You think Stacy's in any danger?"

"Probably not from Tanya. She talks tough, but I doubt she's lethal."

"Boone?"

"Maybe. He's harder to read. Others involved . . . who knows?"

"Somebody besides Rollo? What makes you think that?"

"Tanya knew I was here and where to find me. Somebody local had to tell her. Maybe Rollo, maybe not. And how did he know?"

"She could've seen you on the street or in one of the casinos."

"Possible, I suppose."

"But you don't think so."

"I don't trust coincidence. And I get the feeling that whatever's going on, there's a lot more to it than a simple con game."

"Such as what?"

"Your sister suggested kidnapping."

"My God! With her as the victim?"

"Or her husband. High ransom demand, either way."

"I don't believe it."

"I didn't either, but now I'm not so sure."

"Why would they pick on Stacy and Andy, of all people? And Vince?"

Cape said, "The local angle again. If Rollo's nobody they know, then there has to be somebody else involved. Somebody close enough to one or both of them to have access to those photographs."

"Come on, salesman. No way."

"It's the only answer that makes sense."

"Brrr. Now you're giving me the creeps."

"You know of anyone who might want to harm your sister?"

"You mean like an old boyfriend or somebody else with a grudge? No. Andy, though . . . he's made his share of enemies."

"Anybody in particular?"

"Not that I know about."

"Someone who has it in for both him and Mahannah, maybe."

"You'd have to ask Vince. Don't bother with Andy—he wouldn't tell you."

"Well, it's not up to me," Cape said. "Police are the ones who should be doing the asking."

"Andy won't take your advice and call them. Vince, either."

"No?"

"They don't want anything to do with the law, not if they can help it. Neither of them is what you'd call above reproach in his business dealings, if you catch my drift."

"I catch it."

"Andy's worked more angles than a geometry professor. That's how he made his pile."

"None of my business."

"Stacy says the same thing. Little Miss Ostrich." Lacy sat up, swung one long leg off to the floor. "I need a drink," she said. "You want one?"

"Not just now."

"Be right back."

In the soft lampglow Cape watched her get off the bed, walk languidly across the room. Naked, she had an unusually interesting body. High, up-thrust breasts, fleshy hips, those long slender legs, the largest and thickest patch of pubic hair he'd ever seen on a woman. She liked to show herself off, too. Sultry walk, pause in the doorway, half-profile and then a full frontal view, turn again to exhibit the fluid thrust of her ass as she went through into the living room. Anna had had few inhibitions; Lacy had none. Pure sex, dressed or undressed, vertical or horizontal.

Pretty soon she came back, stood beside the bed looking down at him while she sipped her drink. "No more heavy stuff, okay? Not tonight."

"It's your house and your bed."

She set her glass down, stretched again so her breasts lifted even higher, then lay down and fitted her body against his. Immediately her hand probed between them, clutching, fondling.

"These things fascinate me," she said, "the way they go up and down. As if they have a mind of their own."

"Penis envy."

"Hah. I don't want to own one, just borrow one now and then." Her touch was having the desired effect. "I was nine years old," she said, "the first time I saw one hard."

"Whose was it?"

"My loving daddy's. He raped me with it."

"Jesus, Lacy."

"It happens. More often than you might think."

"You tell anyone?"

"No. He cried afterward, said he was sorry and begged me not to tell anybody. Cry, apologize, beg—he did that every time. Nice as pie when he was sober, a slobbering pig when he was drunk. And he drank a lot, Pops did."

"How long did it go on?"

"Until I was twelve."

"What ended it?"

"He did. With his army forty-five. I guess he hated himself as much as I hated him. I still remember that day—happiest day of my life. If he hadn't done it, I would have myself when I got older. I used to think about killing him all the time, when he was crying and apologizing and begging."

Cape said nothing.

"I don't know if he went after Stacy, too," Lacy said. "Probably, but she won't talk about it. Flat-out refuses."

Still silent.

"Uh-oh, I'm turning you off. Up and now down again."

"Not exactly erotic conversation we're having here," Cape said. "I thought you didn't want any more heavy stuff tonight. Or sex talk in bed."

"Right. Beats me why I told you the deep, dark family secret." Her fingers continued their rhythmic movements, gentle but insistent now. "I'll shut up," she said. "We'll both shut up."

Didn't take her long to make him ready again. She knew plenty of little tricks, only needed a couple of them. She mounted him this time, and she was even noisier, more demanding, almost frenzied. As if she were trying to prove something to herself—that she really did enjoy sex, really did like men, in spite of her father and Joe the Rabbit and the sadomasochist and all the others she'd known and been screwed by and had cause to hate.

* * *

Cape left her shortly past midnight. He didn't ask to spend the night, Lacy didn't issue an invitation. She lay naked on the bed, watching him dress, not saying anything until he was ready to go.

"So when do you leave Tahoe?" she asked then.

"Sunday morning."

"You could come over again tomorrow night."

"Mahannah's poker game. Or didn't I mention that?"

"You mentioned it. I hope you come up winners, but if they take your money early, I'll be here."

"I'll keep it in mind."

"You do that."

He said, "I hope you come up winners, too. In the long run, I mean."

"I will," she said.

"Easy does it?"

"Right. Easy does it, and you make your own luck."

"Not always."

"Often enough." Sleepy cat stretch. "So long, salesman. If I don't see you again, it's been fun."

17

ACY was right about Vanowen and Mahannah. They didn't want anything to do with the law. Voice-mail from Mahannah when Cape got back to the Lakeside Grand. The pair of them had talked it over and they were in agreement: no cops. Don't tell anybody else what happened, Cape. We'll discuss it tomorrow night before the poker game. Get to my place by seven-thirty.

People. But it was their problem; let them handle it their way. He'd done all he could. Come Sunday, he'd be out of it for good.

Quiet Saturday morning in South Lake Tahoe. Cape drove all around the Pioneer Trail/Black Bart Road area, covering an eight-block radius. No blue Mitsubishi. No Tanya, no Boone.

Waste of time. He wasn't even sure why he'd bothered to go over there again. Another encounter with Tanya and her little automatic? Answers to questions that really had nothing much to do with him?

Give it up, Cape. Get on with the rest of your life.

Day trip around the lake. Fallen Leaf Lake, Emerald Bay, Sugar Pine Point, Pine Beach, Homewood, tourist-clogged Tahoe City, Carnelian Bay. Back across the Nevada line and a late lunch in Incline Village. Nevada State Park, a place called Whittell's Castle that sounded interesting but wasn't, Skunk Harbor, Glenwood Bay. Pretty country, but not much different from what he'd already seen coming through the Sierras and driving along the south shore. Restlessness in him now. And the craving for new sights, new experiences, stronger than ever.

He almost regretted accepting Vince Mahannah's invitation to poker tonight. Almost, but not quite.

Mahannah's home in Glenwood north of Cave Rock, like the property of everybody with money in the Tahoe Basin, was big, rustic-styled, lakefront, and private. Cut pine logs, redwood shakes, railed redwood deck, covered walkway leading to a T-shaped concrete pier. Inside, just what you'd expect: redwood paneling, native-stone fireplace, mounted dead-animal heads, Native American rugs and wall hangings, a glass-front gun rack loaded with expensive-looking rifles and shotguns. Forty-foot-square game room overlooking the deck and lake: another stone fireplace, dark brown leather couches and chairs, a wet bar, and in the middle under a green-shaded droplight, an antique poker table, hexagonal, with faded green felt and wells to hold each player's chips.

When Mahannah ushered Cape in there, the man sitting on one of the couches came to his feet as if he were spring-loaded. Andrew Vanowen. Cream-colored cashmere sweater, pearl gray slacks, Gucci loafers—the image of casual elegance. Mahannah's clothes were equally expensive: tailored chinos, a hand-knit shirt. Cape's off-the-rack slacks and pullover seemed tawdry by comparison. Once he would have been a little intimidated in the presence of men like these, surroundings like these. No more.

He acknowledged Vanowen, received a curt nod in return. The drink in Vanowen's hand might have been laced with lemon juice, as tightly puckered as his mouth looked.

Mahannah said to Cape, "Help yourself at the bar."

"No, thanks. I don't drink before I play cards. Or during."

"Is that right? Neither do I."

"I can hold my liquor," Vanowen said argumentatively.

"Sure you can, Andy," Mahannah agreed. "Nothing against you."

Vanowen's narrowed eyes were fixed on Cape. From the flush on his cheeks, he was holding plenty of liquor already. "Enough small talk," he said. "Tell us about the woman, Cape. This Tanya."

"I put the gist of it in my message last night."

"I want to hear you tell it. In detail."

Mahannah said, "Go ahead, humor us."

Cape related the incident, all of it from start to finish. The name Rollo meant nothing to either of them, or so they claimed. "Sounds like a phony name to me," Vanowen said. He was still argumentative; Cape's answers to his questions, more or less the same ones Lacy had asked, didn't seem to satisfy him. He kept digging, kept repeating the same damn questions.

"Now, look," Cape said when he'd had enough. "How many times do I have to say it? I don't have any more idea of what's going on than either of you."

"Don't you?" Vanowen said.

"I just said I didn't."

"Bullshit, Cape. You think we're stupid?"

"Meaning what?"

"Meaning enough game playing." He waved his glass, yanked at his lower lip, shifted his feet, flapped his arms; it was like watching a marionette being manipulated by invisible strings. "Why don't you just go ahead and make your pitch, get it over with."

"*What* pitch?"

Mahannah said in neutral tones, "Andy thinks you're not the good Samaritan you pretend to be. He thinks you have an agenda."

"I think you're looking to shake us down," Vanowen said, "that's what I think."

"Oh, for Christ's sake."

"Look at it from our point of view," Mahannah said reasonably. "You show up in Tahoe with a batch of photographs that no stranger should have in his possession. You tell us an unlikely story about a pair of grifters that can't be corroborated, people we've never seen or heard from even though you say they're now in our backyard. Then you tell us another story that also can't be corroborated about the woman showing up in your hotel room and taking a potshot at you. Wouldn't *you* be suspicious if you were us?"

Cape said, thin and tight, "Come over to the Grand with me, and I'll show you the bullet hole in the carpet."

Pig snort from Vanowen. "That doesn't mean a goddamn thing. You could've put it there yourself."

"For what reason? How is that supposed to help me shake you down?"

"You tell us."

"I'm not going to tell you anything else because there isn't anything else. I don't give a damn what you think or what the Judsons' game is or if one of them walks up someday and shoves you in front of a bus. I've had it. I'm out of here."

He spun on his heel and went.

Mahannah caught up with him as he was pulling the front door open, gripped his arm. Cape fought loose and started out.

"Hold on, will you?"

"Why should I? I'm all through talking to you people."

"Even if I say I don't share Andy's opinions?"

"I don't care if you do or not."

Cape headed across the gravel turnaround to where he'd parked the Corvette. Mahannah hurried after him, swung around between him and the car.

"Cool down, man," he said in his caviar voice. "I mean it—I don't agree with Andy. I think you've been straight with us, down the line."

"Then why side with him in there?"

"I didn't side with him. Just played devil's advocate. You have to admit, it all sounds far-fetched, and there's nothing to back up any of it."

The edge had smoothed off Cape's anger. "Maybe."

"He was the one who was aggressive about it, not me."

"Aggressive, arrogant, offensive. He's a prick."

"I won't give you an argument on that assessment. But I can make him listen to reason, if you'll give me the chance. Let's go back inside, and we'll start over again."

"Give me one good reason why I should."

"I'll give you four," Mahannah said. "The main one is that you'd like to find out what's going on almost as much as we would. If we put our heads together, we might be able to come up with an explanation that makes sense."

"I doubt it."

"Worth a try, just the same."

"Maybe," Cape said again. "The other three reasons?"

"You're already here, you like to gamble, and you don't have anything better to do tonight or you wouldn't have come in the first place."

Cape thought about it. "All right. But if Vanowen gets in my face again, I'm gone for good."

The other players began to arrive at a quarter past eight, were all there by eight-forty. J. T. Sturgess, real-estate developer from South Lake Tahoe. Jack Wineberg, assistant manager of a North Shore casino. Sherman Bellah, owner of one of the local ski resorts. Wayman Jones, freelance writer from Tahoe Keys. All personable types with an obvious passion for poker. Moderate drinkers, nonsmokers—Mahannah evidently had a thing about tobacco, wouldn't allow it in the house—and easy to get along with. The only sour apple in the mix was Vanowen.

But Mahannah had talked to him, and whatever he'd said had had an effect. Vanowen kept his suspicions to himself after that. Nothing came out of their brainstorming except that Vanowen and Mahannah were both adamant about not bringing in the law unless circumstances made it unavoidable.

Cape had relaxed again by the time the six of them grouped around the poker table. It was a warmish night, and Mahannah had the doors to the deck open; Cape's chair faced that way, so that he could see the hard yellow shine of the moon reflected off the lake. Mahannah sat on his right, Bellah on his left, Vanowen across from him.

His kind of game, his kind of players. Very little chatter, no nonsense of any sort. Just good old-fashioned, hard-nosed poker, and the kind of gamesmanship that is mostly friendly but with an edge. That was something else they all shared, a passion for winning. Not a loser in the bunch. Even Vanowen played his cards close, with complete concentration.

Two large pots in the first half-dozen hands. Cape stayed in both, lost both. Sturgess and Mahannah pushed him, testing his mettle, trying to read his game. He didn't show them any more than they showed him. Wineberg tried to bluff him on another hand; Cape won it with a pair of sixes to Wineberg's treys. They treated him as an equal after that.

Fast game, intense but not cutthroat, high-stakes betting but not the variety that would have driven Cape out unless he hit an early streak. He didn't hit a streak; he lost sixteen hundred in the first hour. He didn't change his game, continuing to bet aggressively when a hand warranted it, and finally he began to draw better cards. He won two hands of five-stud in a row, lost one, then claimed a twenty-eight-hundred-dollar pot with an ace-high spade flush over Wineberg's trip kings and Vanowen's small straight. That earned him a laser glare across the table. Vanowen hated to lose, and so far it wasn't his night.

Three hours in, Mahannah and Jones were the big winners, and Cape had edged up to twenty-one hundred ahead. Vanowen had won just one small pot, was down close to five thousand and letting it get to him. Every time he lost or folded now, he turned his glare on Cape as if holding him personally responsible. He took to getting up every few minutes and refilling his glass at the wet bar. The others noted it, but nobody said anything except Mahannah.

"Night's young, Andy. Why not go easy on that stuff?"

"I don't need any lectures on drinking."

"I wasn't delivering one. Just making a comment."

"Well, keep your comments to yourself."

Vanowen finally won another pot, a good-size one, but it didn't seem to improve his mood. He was still glowering, still drinking. The deal passed to him, and he slapped out a hand of seven-stud. Cape's hole cards were a king and a jack, his first up card another jack. Promising. He bet the pair, caught a third jack on the next round, bet accordingly. Vanowen, with a pair of tens, raised him a hundred; Cape upped that another hundred, got a call and another glare in return.

Vanowen picked up the deck to deal the next round. And all at once, he froze and the glower metamorphosed into a stare of astonishment. He said explosively, "Jesus Christ!"

A couple of the others made startled noises, their eyes raised to something behind Cape. He swiveled his head, then froze himself.

Somebody had come into the room, breeze-silent, and was now moving quickly toward the table. Five or six inches under six feet, compact, dressed all in black, head covered by a black ski mask, one hand waggling a large-caliber automatic.

"Everybody sit still, you don't want to die." Raspy, nervous male voice muffled by the mask. "Hands on the table. Do it!"

They did it. The sudden tension in the room was electric. Cape could feel it on the back of his neck, prickling, stiffening the short hairs.

The gunman took something white and folded from his pocket, moved close enough to toss it on the table. Pillowcase or flour sack. "You," he said to Sturgess, who was the bank. "Fill it with the cash. Hurry up."

Vanowen opened his mouth. "You won't get away with this."

"Shut up."

"You think we don't know who you are? Even with that mask?"

Cape glanced over at him. Veins bulged in his neck, throbbed in his temples. His liquor-shiny eyes showed anger, contempt, but no fear.

"I told you shut up, asshole." The automatic made fidgety, weaving motions; to Cape it was like watching a coiled, one-eyed snake. "Rest of you put your wallets, watches, jewelry on the table. Everything valuable. Use one hand, keep the other where I can see it."

Silently, they complied. Vanowen was the only one who took his time, and when he had his wallet out, he slapped it down hard on the felt. The platinum ring on his left hand, with its circle of fat diamonds, made gleams and glints in the spill from the low-hanging droplight. Instead of stripping it off, he covered it with his other hand.

"Everything in the sack," the gunman said to Sturgess. And when it was full, "Pass it over to this guy here," indicating Cape.

Cape took the sack.

"Hold it out with your right hand."

He did that, and the gunman came forward and snatched it from him. Backed off again.

"You," he said, and now he was looking at Vanowen. "That ring you're covering up. Take it off, toss it over here."

Vanowen sat motionless, glaring.

"Take it off. Now!"

"Go to hell, Judson. That's what you call yourself, isn't it?"

Mahannah said warningly, "Andy, for God's sake."

"Boone Judson. You—"

The masked man shot him. In the face, so that Vanowen's head seemed to burst in streaks and spatters of bright red.

The automatic shifted and he fired again, this time straight at Cape.

18

CAPE was already moving in a sideways dive out of the chair. The bullet missed close, burning through the left side of his shirt. He jarred into the floor, his legs tangled up with the chair. He heard the gun go off again, and in the same instant the poker table came crashing down on top of him. That round missed, too; the metal jacket thwacked into something solid near his head.

All around him was chaos. Moans, yells, running steps, scrambling on the hardwood floor, the air choked with the stink of burned powder. An edge of the table dug into his back; somebody's flailing elbow cracked the side of his jaw as he heaved up. The weight shifted off him. He kicked loose of the chair, corkscrewed his body around. One hand slicked through something wet and sticky as he dragged his knees under him and shoved, lurching, to his feet.

For a second or two his vision was cockeyed. When it cleared, he saw that the shooter was no longer in the game room. The running steps . . . he could still hear them in another part of the house. Heading for the front entrance? He ran that way, not looking back even when somebody yelled his name, the commotion made by the others diminishing behind him.

The front door stood wide open. He plunged outside. Powdery moonlight brightened the gravel turnaround, gleamed off the dark shapes of cars; nobody moved anywhere among them. The access drive and the road beyond were empty black stripes. Then his ears picked up rustlings, the snap and crackle of twigs being crushed: the gunman was somewhere in the woods that stretched along the lakeshore. Cape ran parallel to the house and the railed deck, across the far edge of the turnaround. Over there was a path angling away into the evergreens. Enough moonshine filtered down through the overhead branches to soften shadows, give him a sense of where he was going.

Sudden noise: engine starting up somewhere ahead.

He couldn't move any faster in the darkness. Twice he almost blundered into the boles of trees. A narrow little inlet materialized on his right, then a wooded finger of land. Beyond the finger the engine noise rose, steadied, began to thread away. Boat of some kind leaving the shore.

He stumbled on until the hard yellow-and-black gleam of the lake appeared again. Another inlet, a circlet of mud-and-sand beach fringed with mashed-down ferns and scrub, a furrow in the damp earth to show where the boat had been drawn up out of the water. And out on the lake, a couple of hundred yards distant now, moving fast on a southwesterly course, an indistinct shape that was the boat itself. Seconds later, as Cape stood there panting, the shape vanished beyond another slender wooded peninsula.

In the new hush he heard thrashings in the woods behind him. Then a shout: "Cape! Where the hell are you?" Mahannah's voice. He turned to see flashlight beams throwing crazy patterns of light and shadow among the trees. Not answering the hail, he stood there waiting.

Mahannah burst into sight first, torch in one hand, a shotgun from his gun cabinet clenched in the other. Sturgess and Wineberg were with him, neither man armed.

"Where'd he go?" Mahannah demanded.

"Out on the lake. He had a power boat waiting here."

Sturgess said, "You took a chance, running after him like that. He might've shot you too."

"He tried hard enough inside. Those last two rounds were aimed at me."

Cape stepped past the others, started back along the path. After a few seconds they trooped after him. Mahannah came up alongside, lighting the way with his flashlight, but he had nothing more to say just yet. Neither did Cape.

Inside, Bellah and Jones were perched on one of the couches, big snifters of cognac in their hands, both white-faced and wearing stunned expressions. A sheet had been found and used to shroud the body of Andrew Vanowen. Blood stained it over what was left of the dead face. The poker table still lay on its side, chips and cards, shattered glass and streaks of blood, littering the floor around it and the sheeted mound.

Jones stirred and said to Mahannah, "We had to cover him. His head . . . the blood . . ."

"One of you notify the county sheriff?"

"I did," Bellah said. "They're on the way."

Cape made a detour to the wet bar. Reaction had set in; his head ached, his legs felt jellied. When he leaned for support on the bar, he noticed a coagulating red smear on his palm. Vanowen's blood. He went around behind the bar, washed his hands in the sink there.

Jones was saying, "Window in your bedroom's open, Vince. Must be how the bastard got inside."

"How'd he know about the game?" Wineberg asked rhetorically. "We don't advertise when we're playing."

"Never mind that. Why in God's name did he kill poor Andy?"

Cape helped himself to a slug of cognac.

Sturgess said, "Andy recognized him, that's why. Said his name just before he was shot. What was it . . . Johnson?"

"Judson," Mahannah said. "Boone Judson."

"Right. But who the hell is Judson? How'd Andy know him?"

Mahannah turned to look at Cape. His slick, handsome face was set in grim lines, his gaze no longer friendly.

"No," Cape said.

"What do you mean, 'no'?"

"He didn't kill Vanowen because he was recognized. That's not why he fired those last two rounds at me, either."

"What're you talking about?"

"When he stepped forward and took the sack out of my hand, I got a good look at his eyes through the mask holes. They were brown."

"So?"

"Judson's eyes are blue," Cape said. "Whoever the gunman is, he's not Boone Judson."

19

NSIDE of an hour, the house and property were swarming with Douglas County sheriff's personnel. The man in charge was a plainclothes captain named D'Anzello. Mid-forties, big without being fat, deceptively soft-spoken and slow-moving; mop of black hair, bushy salt-and-pepper mustache. Efficient, professional. The kind of man who doesn't have to say or do much to command respect or attention, whose presence in a room is enough to make him its focal point.

D'Anzello asked preliminary questions to get an overview of what had happened. Then he took them one by one into Mahannah's study, while the rest waited their turn in the main living room. Mahannah was the first. So Cape knew he'd be second even before he was called.

The study had the same determinedly masculine look as the rest of the house, dominated by a desk of some polished wood whose color matched the redwood paneling. D'Anzello hadn't appropriated the desk. Both he and a second, younger plainclothesman were on their feet, waiting in the middle of the room.

D'Anzello said, "Sit down, Mr. Cape."

"I'd rather stand, if you don't mind."

"Suit yourself. Matthew Cape, is that right?"

"Yes."

"Current residence?"

"Lakeside Grand in Stateline."

"Current permanent residence?"

"I don't have one. Mahannah must've told you that."

"Last place you lived for more than a week or two?"

"Rockford, Illinois. Born there, lived there all my life until a few weeks ago."

"What happened a few weeks ago?"

Cape told him, keeping it terse.

"So now you just travel around the country, living out of a suitcase. The vagabond life."

"That's one term for it."

"Finance this lifestyle how?"

"Savings, mostly."

"Supplemented by gambling winnings?"

"Not really. I like to gamble, but it's only a hobby."

"High-stakes poker?"

"When I can afford it. The game tonight was about my limit."

The other sheriff's investigator had a tape recorder going and was making written notes besides. That was all he was there for, to make sure they got everything they might need. D'Anzello did all the talking.

"Ever been in trouble before?" he asked.

"Gambling trouble? No."

"Any kind of trouble."

"Kid stuff in Rockford."

"What kind of kid stuff?"

"Possession of marijuana when I was fifteen. Charge was dropped."

"Still smoke dope, do you, Mr. Cape?"

"No."

"Use any other kind of drugs?"

"No."

"What about adult trouble? With the law, I mean."

"None."

"Not even a speeding ticket?"

"Not even a parking ticket," Cape said.

"We'll check on that, you know."

"Go right ahead. The closest to adult trouble I've had was a month or so ago in New Orleans. I happened to witness a purse-snatching, chased the thief, caught him, and held him until the law got there. You can check on that, too."

"We will," D'Anzello said. "Let's move on to your reasons for being in this area."

"Mahannah must've filled you in on that."

"I'd like to hear it from you."

Cape's smile was faint, wry. "You know how tired I am of telling this story?"

"A man was murdered here tonight, Mr. Cape," D'Anzello said in sharper tones. "Tell the story one more time, and don't leave anything out."

"Sure. One more time."

When he was done, D'Anzello said, "Let's see if I have this straight. You took the satchelful of money from the Judsons and just let them walk away scot-free."

"That's right."

"Why? They'd run this scam on you and the conventioneers—professional cardsharps certain to keep on fleecing other innocent people. If you're such a good Samaritan, why didn't you report them to the San Francisco police, take them out of commission?"

"I never said I was a good Samaritan. I don't put that label on myself."

"What label would you put on yourself?"

"None. I wore one for too many years in Rockford."

"Answer the question. Why didn't you go to the police?"

"It would've meant hanging around there for days, maybe longer. I didn't want to get that involved."

"You drove up here with those photographs. Got yourself involved with Mahannah and the Vanowens."

"They're not the main reason I came to Tahoe," Cape said. "I like to gamble, I told you that."

"So delivering the photos and telling about the Judsons was an incidental good deed."

"If you want to put it that way."

"Like divvying up the sixteen thousand among the other marks."

"Not so incidental in that case."

"You didn't think for a minute about keeping the entire sixteen thousand? After all, who'd've known except the Judsons? And they weren't in a position to do anything about it."

"I'm not a thief," Cape said. "It was the other players' money, they'd been cheated the same as I had. If you don't believe I returned it to them, I'll give you their names, and you can get their addresses from the hotels and ask them."

D'Anzello said mildly, "Maybe you just had bigger fish to fry."

"Meaning what?"

"The Vanowens and Vince Mahannah. Using those photos to worm your way into their good graces, get yourself an invitation to the private game tonight."

"Is that what you think?"

"I don't think anything. Yet."

"I had no idea who the people in those photos were when I came here."

"Might've been something else in the satchel to identify them."

"There wasn't."

"So you say. But we only have your word for that, don't we."

"And I suppose I knew about Mahannah's private game in advance, too. Also from something in the satchel."

"It's possible."

"I didn't invite myself here tonight," Cape said. Hammer-pound in his head now, a gnawing queasiness in his gut. "Mahannah issued the invitation. Ask him."

"I already did. If he hadn't invited you, you could've been ready to manipulate him into it."

"To set up what happened here tonight, is that what you're getting at?"

"The robbery, yes. Another possibility."

"Me and the gunman in cahoots. Crap."

"Mr. Vanowen identified him as Boone Judson just before he was shot. Everyone agrees to that."

"Well, he was mistaken. The right body type, but Judson has blue eyes and the gunman had brown eyes. I told the others that before you got here. And he wasn't wearing contact lenses, if that's what you're thinking. There's no good reason for Judson or whoever the real gunman was to try to change his eye color."

"That isn't what I was thinking," D'Anzello said.

"No?"

"No. What I'm thinking is that we have only your word, your unsubstantiated word, about the color of Judson's eyes. Or anything else about him."

"So what's your scenario, then? Vanowen was killed because the gunman panicked at being recognized?"

"Makes sense that way."

"He wasn't Boone Judson," Cape said. He had to struggle to keep a tight rein on his temper. "And his last two shots were meant for me. Look at the burn hole in my shirt, if you don't believe me. If I was his partner, why would he want to take me out?"

"Pretty obvious, isn't it? He had the loot in hand, and with you dead he wouldn't have to split it. Kill one, kill two."

"You're wrong, Captain. Dead wrong."

"Then give me a better explanation. Who's the shooter, if not Judson?"

"Somebody with a boat. Somebody who knows the lake well enough to find this place in the dark, and stoned besides. Somebody local."

"Stoned?"

"The way he kept fidgeting, the sound of his voice. And his pupils were dilated."

"Then how could you tell they were brown?"

"Dilated, not invisible. They were brown, all right."

"Why didn't you tell us this before?"

"I didn't have a chance. You kept me too busy with questions about my personal history."

D'Anzello didn't like that. But he said only, "If Vanowen's ID was wrong, why was he shot?"

"I don't know."

"Why did Judson and the woman—Tanya, is it?—have the photographs in the first place? Why did they come to Tahoe? Why was she so scared when she showed up in your room at the Grand? How did she know where to find you? What's their connection to what happened here tonight?"

"Same answer to every question. I don't know."

"All you know is what you've told us, what you've been telling everybody all along."

"That's right. And you can't prove any different."

"Can't we?"

"No, because it's God's honest truth."

"We'll see about that."

Cape said, "More questions, or can I leave now?"

"This room, but not the premises. We'll tell you when."

"I'd like to get some sleep."

"Wouldn't we all," D'Anzello said. When Cape turned for the door, he added, "Once you get back to the Grand, better make arrangements for an extended stay. You understand?"

Bitterly: "Yeah, I understand."

"Cooperation goes a long way with me, Mr. Cape. It helps me stay focused on a man as innocent until proven guilty, instead of the other way around."

"Don't worry, I'll be available when you want to talk to me again."

Available. Another word for trapped.

Three A.M. before they let him leave. Cape was in the 'Vette, the engine rumbling, warming up, when Mahannah came rushing out of the house and leaned down to the driver's window. It was the first chance he'd had for private words with Cape since the law's arrival; the way he hissed them out, they'd been building in him like gas.

"If you had anything to do with this, Cape, by God I'll make you sorry you were ever born."

"I didn't."

"Even if not, you're still partly to blame."

"How do you figure that?"

"Showing up here, putting all of us on edge. None of this might've happened if you'd stayed the hell away from Lake Tahoe."

"Odds on the robbery would've gone down whether I was at the table tonight or not."

"So you say. I don't like those odds."

Cape made no reply.

Parting shot from Mahannah: "Innocent or guilty, Cape, you're bad luck. You're a walking pair of snake eyes."

20

No sleep. Too keyed up.

He kept going over it in the clinging darkness. Dead ends, angles that wouldn't connect to other angles. Like trying to work up a sales pitch with half the facts and figures missing.

Mahannah's last words to him added up, though. About the only thing that did.

Bad-luck Cape.

Cape, the walking pair of snake eyes.

Somewhere past six he finally slept. Two hours or so, that was all. He woke up groggy, aching in his joints, soaked in sweat. A long shower didn't make him feel much better.

Before he left the room he called Visa and MasterCard to report that his credit cards had been stolen. Downstairs, he made arrangements for a lengthier stay at the Grand. He'd left a thousand dollars in the hotel safe before heading out to Mahannah's last night; he claimed three hundred of it now. Four thousand gone in the robbery, along with his wallet and cards. If D'Anzello didn't open up his box pretty soon, he'd have to arrange with a local bank for a transfer of funds from his Rockford account. Losing the money was bad enough. Losing his freedom for an indefinite period was a hell of a lot worse.

The day stretched ahead of him, long and empty.

✳ ✳ ✳

Pioneer Trail, Black Bart Road.

Nothing. Grabbing at straws, pissing in the wind.

Cave Rock.

Lacy wasn't home. He drove around, drove around, stopped at a café and forced himself to eat something, returned to her dog-vomit house on Lake Summit Road. Still not home.

Back to the Lakeside Grand? No. Mahannah's house, see if he was there and what his mood was today? Not yet, not this soon.

That left Rubicon Bay.

The gates were open at the entrance to the Vanowen property. When Cape reached the bottom of the curving drive, he had the parking area to himself. But a car was drawn up under the carport: silver BMW, the same one as in the photo of Stacy Vanowen.

No answer at the door. Cape followed a path that led around the house and down toward the boathouse. At the rear the path branched, its shorter arm leading to a gated terrace—broad, rectangular, balustraded with peeled-bark logs, extending out a few feet over the lake on thick pilings. On the terrace were several pieces of white tubular furniture, an open-fronted redwood hutch that served as an outdoor bar. And Stacy Vanowen, sitting alone at an umbrella-shaded table, staring out across the sunstruck water.

Cape went to the terrace gate. Hot back here in the open; temperature must be close to ninety today. The early-afternoon sun was like a heat pad on the back of his neck. Quiet here, too: faint boat thrummings from the lake, an onshore wind making rustling, crying sounds in the tops of the pines.

"Mrs. Vanowen?" He had to say it again before his voice penetrated. Her head snapped around; she flipped up the dark glasses she wore.

"Oh . . . it's you."

"I didn't mean to startle you. I rang the bell—"

"I didn't hear it. What do you want?"

"To talk to you briefly. Offer my condolences."

No response.

"Okay if I come in for a minute or two?"

"... Yes. All right."

She lowered the shades again, so he couldn't see her eyes as he approached the table. But her attitude was wary, as if she wasn't sure whether or not to be afraid of him. She wore shorts, a loose Hawaiian-style shirt, sandals. Face composed, without makeup or evidence of grief. The table beside her was bare of any sorrow-drowning substance.

"I'm sorry about your husband, Mrs. Vanowen."

"Yes. Everybody is. The police. Vince. The phone ... it keeps ringing. That's one of the reasons I came out here, to get away from the phone. You can only listen to people being sorry for so long."

"I understand."

"Do you?"

"You'd rather be alone. I won't stay long."

"I do and I don't," she said. She tilted her head back to look at him. "Vince thinks you might've had something to do with what happened."

"He's wrong."

"He says you won't get away with it if you did."

"Whoever's responsible won't get away with it. The law will see to that."

"Who *is* responsible? Those people, the Judsons?"

"They're mixed up in it somehow," Cape said. "But Boone Judson wasn't the man in the ski mask."

"You're certain of that?"

"Positive."

"Every time I try to think about it, it just ... my head starts to hurt. Confusing, senseless. Andy ... he—"

"He didn't suffer," Cape said, "if that helps."

"It doesn't. He's gone, and I'm here, I *am* suffering. Not only because of the way he died, because I—"

"Yes?"

"Never mind. It's none of your business." She looked out over the lake again. "I wish I was out there right now," she said.

"On the water?"

"Far out, in the middle. Away from here."

"Where people being sorry can't get at you."

"People, pressures, things that hurt," she said. "Out there, it's like you're on an island all your own. That's the real appeal of boats, you know."

"Floating islands. Safe havens."

"Exactly." Her gaze shifted to him again. "Do you know anything about boats, Mr. Cape? Boat engines?"

"A little about engines in general."

"Can you fix one that won't start?"

"Depends on the problem."

Abruptly, she was on her feet. "Come with me."

He followed her off the terrace, down to the boathouse. Fast walker, Stacy Vanowen, hips rolling and long legs scissoring. Legs as long and strong and nicely formed as her sister's. Cape looked at them, looked away. Legs that belonged to a brand-new widow. If he closed his eyes, he could still see the image of Andrew Vanowen's exploding face.

Cool, gloomy inside the boathouse. She flipped on an overhead light. Two berths, each outfitted with a curve-armed electric hoist, but only one boat sat in the placid water. A seventeen-foot, four-seat Sportliner inboard, sleek and low-slung. The housing was off the engine, an open toolbox beside it.

"It turns over, but it won't start," she said. "I looked at it, but . . . I don't understand mechanical things very well."

Cape stepped over into the stern, squatted to peer into the engine well. Powerful four-cylinder job, well cared for. It took him less than a minute to locate the problem, another minute to repair it with a wrench and a screwdriver from the toolbox.

"Loose ignition wire," he explained to Stacy Vanowen.

"Will it start now?"

"We'll find out."

He swung over behind the wheel. Key was in the slot. On the first try the engine farted, caught, choked off. On the second it caught easily, steadied into a low rumbling purr.

"Leave it running or shut it off?"

"Leave it running. I want to take her out right now."

"Mind if I go along?"

"Why?"

"I feel like a safe haven myself right now."

"I may want to stay out for a couple of hours or more."

"I don't have anything else to do this afternoon."

"All right," she said. "I guess I really don't want to be alone, even out on the lake."

She knew her way around boats. Quickly she maneuvered the Sportliner out of the slip and into open water, fed the engine a little gas, then slammed the throttle all the way forward. The sudden acceleration threw Cape back hard against the seat. The wind hit them head-on, hurling spray back over the upthrust bow and the windshield; it stung icily on his cheeks and bare arms.

They went straight out from shore, running wide open, the beat of the pistons loud in his ears, the boat airborne between bucking, skimming bounces on the wind-ruffled water. Stacy Vanowen handled the wheel easily, body relaxed, hair like a fan of gold shining in the sun, spray glistening on her smooth-marble face. Exhilaration built in Cape—the speed, the wind, the throbbing power beneath him, the alternation of soaring weightlessness and jarring, gliding impact. More danger, greater thrill in a skydiving freefall, but the sensations were similar. Competition racing would be like this—boats, cars. He'd have to try one or the other of those sports, or both. As soon as he was free again.

Ten minutes or more of headlong flight, then Stacy Vanowen cut back to half throttle, shut it all the way down a few seconds later. The Sportliner skimmed and settled, began to drift once she switched off the ignition. Cape wiped his face, turned to look back the way they'd come. The distant shoreline was a series of scalloped fingers and bays, wooded mountain slopes and snow-capped crests. Buildings were dots of various sizes on the green-and-brown background, like pins jabbed into a topographical map.

He said, "You always push it like that?"

"Sometimes. When I need to get away badly enough. Did it bother you, the speed?"

"On the contrary."

"It makes me feel alive," she said.

"Same here. The faster you travel, the more alive you feel."

There was less wind this far out, and now that they were no longer moving, the sun's heat became a weight again. She felt it, too; she unfolded a half-awning to shade the front seats.

"Floating island," Cape said.

"For a while. Then we'll run again."

"Where to?"

"Anywhere. Nowhere. It's a big lake—ten miles long, twenty-eight miles wide. We're not even close to the middle here."

"So I see."

"It's deep, too. In the middle."

"How deep?"

"Fifteen hundred feet. I wonder what it's like on the bottom out there, fifteen hundred feet down."

"Dark," Cape said.

"And cold," she said. "Cold as the grave."

She leaned back, closed her eyes. For a time Cape alternated between watching her and glancing up at the sky and mountains, out across the water. There was just enough breeze to turn the boat this way and that, changing his perspective slightly each time.

"Can we talk a little, Mrs. Vanowen?"

"Stacy," she said. "I'm not Mrs. Vanowen anymore."

"Whatever you prefer."

"Talk about what?"

"What happened last night."

"Why? I don't understand it, you say you don't."

"Not yet, but I'm trying."

"Just thinking about it makes my head hurt—I told you that."

"He tried to kill me, too," Cape said. "The man who murdered your husband."

Her eyes popped open, slanting toward him. "You can't be sure of that."

"I can be, and I am. His last two shots were meant for me."

"Why would he try to kill you?"

"Why did he kill your husband?"

"He thought Andy recognized him—"

"He isn't Boone Judson. Why shoot a man who identifies you as somebody else?"

"I don't know. . . . I suppose he panicked. A common thief . . ."

"He didn't panic," Cape said. "He was high on drugs, fidgety, but he knew what he was doing the entire time. And I'm not so sure he was a common thief."

"What do you mean by that?"

"Robbery may not have been his real motive."

She sat up, facing him now. "What're you saying?"

"I'm not saying anything. Just speculating."

"You . . . my God, you can't think what he did to Andy was *deliberate?*"

"It may've been. Your husband had a lot of enemies, I've been told."

"Not that kind of enemy. Andy was a businessman, he dealt with large companies, intelligent, sane people. The kind of thing you're implying . . . well, it's unthinkable."

"Not necessarily. The person responsible could be clever, ruthless, loaded with hate."

"What person? What are you saying now?"

"I don't think Rollo acted alone."

"Rollo? Where did you get that name?"

"From Tanya Judson. Odds are he's the man in the ski mask." Disbelieving stare.

"You don't know anyone by that name?" he asked her.

"No."

"Never heard your husband or anyone else use it?"

"No. What did Tanya Judson tell you about this Rollo person?"

"Nothing much. Just that he and Boone were involved in whatever scheme brought Judson to Tahoe."

"Now I suppose you want me to believe three people, three strangers, are mixed up in a deliberate plot to murder my husband?"

"Three or more. And at least one of them may not be a stranger."

"That's ridiculous."

"For your sake, I hope you're right."

"You didn't know Andy, you don't know anything about his business or his private life." Vein of contempt in her voice now. "How can you make such irresponsible accusations?"

"Informed guesses, not accusations."

"They're still irresponsible. If the masked man was there to . . . to murder Andy, why would he try to shoot you?"

"Maybe because somebody thinks I know too much."

"It's all just one huge conspiracy, is that it? Now you sound paranoid."

Cape said, "How well do you know Vince Mahannah?"

". . . What?"

"Well enough to have an affair with him?"

"How dare you!"

"It's pretty obvious how he feels about you. Question is, how far would he go to make a relationship with you permanent?"

Withering glare. For a second or two, she seemed poised to lean over and slap him. Instead she swung around, twisted the ignition key, slammed the throttle forward. She brought the boat around in such a tight turn it came close to capsizing before she regained control.

No more free running on the lake. No more conversation. Straight back to the Vanowen property, bouncing and hydroplaning at warp speed all the way.

21

COMPANY waiting on the Vanowen terrace. Indistinct figure in the distance . . . dark-haired woman in a white pants suit . . . Lacy. As they slowed coming in, she walked down onto the dock. She stood watching her sister maneuver the Sportliner along the side opposite the boathouse, making no move to help tie off the bow and stern lines. Cape stepped up and did the job himself.

Lacy said, "Hello, salesman. Fancy meeting you here," and turned away before he could frame a response.

Stacy Vanowen shut off the engine, climbed up onto the dock. Her face was still set in pinched, angry lines.

"Is this a private wake," Lacy said to her, "or can I join in?"

"Lacy, please. You're not funny."

"You don't seem exactly grief-stricken yourself."

"How would you know? You've never had anyone to mourn."

"Never had anyone worth mourning. Why didn't you call me about Andy? Nobody bothers to tell me anything. I had to find out about it on the radio, an hour ago."

"If I had called, I suppose you'd've rushed right over to hold my hand."

"I might have. We'll never know, will we."

"Don't pretend you care that much. You never liked poor Andy."

"No, I didn't. *De mortuis* and all that, but he was a bastard."

"For God's sake!"

"Well? Don't you pretend, either, little sister. We both know you didn't like him a whole lot yourself."

"That's not true. I loved him."

"Once, maybe. I'll bet you won't miss him any more than I will."

Stacy Vanowen glared at her, transferred the glare briefly to Cape, and stalked away to the house.

Cape said, "Little hard on her, weren't you?"

"If there's one thing I hate," Lacy said, "it's a hypocrite. You want the truth? She'd've divorced Andy years ago if it weren't for his money."

"Little sister, weak sister?"

"In spades. So why didn't *you* call or come by and give me the news?"

"I drove over mid-morning. You weren't home."

"I had to go to Reno. It happened last night, not this morning."

"Three A.M. by the time the law let me leave Mahannah's. I didn't feel much like talking to anybody else. Even you."

"Good enough excuse, I guess. It's not every night you see a man get his face shot off."

"Or almost have the same thing happen to you."

"How's that again?"

Cape explained.

"Heavy," Lacy said. "You sure he wasn't just shooting at random?"

"I was the target, all right. First Vanowen, then me."

"What do you mean?"

"I think it was deliberate. Premeditated."

"Are you serious? Why would somebody want both of you dead?"

"If I knew the answer to that, I wouldn't be here."

"Come on, salesman. It was a robbery gone bad. That's what the radio said."

"You believe everything you hear on the radio?"

"Andy was a prick, sure. The more you knew him, the less you liked him. But murder? And you haven't been here long enough to piss anybody off that way. I don't buy it."

"I won't try to sell it to you then," Cape said. "Why was he a prick?"

"Let me count the ways. Fast and loose with other people's

money, arrogant, vain, a control freak, and a serial fornicator. He propositioned me once at a party. Had his hand halfway up my skirt while he was whispering in my ear."

"What'd you do?"

"Told him to go screw himself. He just laughed. Rejection never bothered him. There was always another woman around who'd say yes."

"You tell your sister?"

"No point. She wouldn't have cared much."

"Why not? Sleep around herself?"

Lacy shrugged.

Cape said, "With Vince Mahannah, for instance?"

"You're pretty nosy, you know that? Why don't you ask her?"

"I did, out on the lake."

"I'll bet she didn't give you a straight answer."

"You win the bet."

"What were you doing out there with her, anyway?"

"She wanted to go for a ride," Cape said. "Engine wouldn't start, and I fixed it. She let me go along for company."

"Chummy."

"She didn't want to be alone, she said."

"She didn't look too happy with you just now. The Mahannah question? Or did you come on to her, offer her a sympathy fuck?"

"You know something, lady? Your sister was right. You're not funny today."

Wry mouth and another shrug. "I'm not funny most days," she said. Then, "He's in love with her, you know."

"Mahannah? I figured as much. How does she feel about him?"

"Oh, Christ, all right, I might as well tell you. They had an affair. Hot and heavy for a while, then it cooled off. Now . . . maybe she's still sleeping with him, maybe she's not. Like I told you before, she doesn't confide in me. All my information is reliable enough, but second- or thirdhand."

"What cooled off the affair?"

"Andy found out about it. Bruised his big male ego that the goose was also getting some on the side. From what I understand he threatened to throw her out if she didn't break it off with Vince."

"The money mean that much to her?"

"Their prenup did," Lacy said. "He insisted on one when they were married. She wouldn't have collected a dime in a divorce action."

"How about now that she's a widow?"

"She gets everything. What're you thinking, salesman? That she had something to do with Andy's murder so she could inherit as his widow?"

"It's been known to happen."

"Not with Little Miss Priss. She's afraid of her own shadow, or hadn't you noticed? She doesn't have enough guts to step on a bug."

"Mahannah strikes me as the bug-squashing type."

"What, the two of them working together? Oh, man!"

"Did Vanowen also confront Mahannah when he found out about the affair?"

"That I don't know," Lacy said. "I doubt it. Why?"

"If he did, threatened him, maybe, it'd give Mahannah another reason to want him out of the way."

"Sure. And what's his motive for wanting *you* out of the way? Salesman, you're so full of shit I can't stand to be downwind of you."

He said nothing.

"Robbery gone bad," Lacy said. "That's what it was, that's all it was. You can't make it into anything else. Why don't you just count yourself lucky and walk away?"

"I can't."

"That target crap, I suppose?"

"Partly."

"What else? The money you lost? It couldn't've been that much—"

"Money's not an issue."

"Then what is?"

"My freedom," Cape said. "The law thinks I had something to do with setting up the robbery."

Raised eyebrow. "You didn't, did you?"

"No. But I'm stuck here until they realize it."

"Poor baby. What's a few days out of your life?"

"A hell of a lot if days turn into weeks and you're running low on funds."

"So get a job for the duration. I know a pit boss at Harrah's. He'd put you on as a dealer if I asked him."

Again Cape was silent.

"Beneath you? I guess you'd prefer a nice, cushy sales job in-stead."

He said, "Not funny at all today," and turned away from her.

"Look me up if you change your mind."

He stopped, glanced back. "How about if I get lonely? Feel the need of some TLC?"

"Uh-uh. You had all you're going to get from me."

"You seemed to like it well enough the other night."

"That was the other night. This is now. So long, salesman."

Snake eyes again.

22

MAHANNAH.

Not home. Sheriff's deputy on guard to keep the morbidly curious away from the crime scene. The deputy had no idea where Mahannah had gone.

D'Anzello.

In his office in Carson City, and willing to talk. But not willing to bend.

"I can't tell you yet how long you'll have to stay in the area, Mr. Cape. We don't get many homicide cases in this county, and when we do, they take time and patience."

"For you, but why for me?"

"There's no place you have to be, is there? Nothing urgent on your agenda?"

"That's not the point. I tell you, I'm not involved in what happened last night."

"Then we'll confirm that eventually, and you can be on your way."

"At least tell me if you're making any progress so far."

"Some."

"What kind?"

"I can't go into details," D'Anzello said. "But I will tell you this.

Your man Boone Judson has a felony record that includes prison terms in New Jersey and Arizona."

"He's not my man. And I'm not surprised."

"Mostly fraud connected with gambling scams, but one conviction was for armed assault. Short step from there to armed robbery and murder."

"You really think he'd take that step throwing his own name around?"

"He used his name in San Francisco, you said, not in connection with anybody up here. Besides, only some career criminals use an alias. Most of them are egomaniacs and not very smart."

"Would I have told you his real name if I was mixed up with him and his goddamn scheme?"

"You might if you thought it would make you look innocent."

Cape said wearily, "I am innocent. And Judson wasn't the man in the ski mask. How many times do I have to say it?"

"Until we can prove otherwise. Go back to Tahoe, Mr. Cape. Relax, enjoy the attractions the area has to offer. I'll contact you when the time comes, one way or another."

Relax, enjoy. Bullshit.

Plenty of options, all right, but none of them had any appeal.

Stay in Carson City.

Check out Reno.

Return to Stateline.

Prowl the Pioneer Trail/Black Bart Road section again.

Gamble.

Get drunk.

Find a quiet church to sit in.

Give Justine another try.

Sit in his room, stare at the four walls until they started to close in on him.

He didn't make a conscious decision, except to take Highway 50 back through the mountains to Tahoe. Late afternoon by the time he reached Stateline, and he hadn't eaten all day. Hunger pangs and swarming weekend crowds sent him over into South Lake Tahoe. He stopped at the first place he saw, a brew pub, and swallowed a sandwich and a couple of beers.

Back into the 'Vette, more restless than ever. Dry salt taste in his mouth from the barbecued sandwich meat. Neon bar sign ahead; another stop, another beer. Then he knew what he was going to do.

Pub crawl.

He'd done it before when he was feeling this way, in New Orleans and Oklahoma and the Texas border towns. Hunt up a tavern, beer or two in each, some conversation if there was anybody worth talking to, and on to the next place. Part of the game was that each one had to be a little seedier than the last. Not looking for trouble, just moving and soaking up native atmosphere. Like descending through levels of rock strata until you had a good look at what was crawling around on the bottom.

The bottom of South Lake Tahoe was at the southwest end, beyond the junction of Highways 50 and 89. Semi-industrial, trailer parks, taverns with barred windows. The Hip-Hop Bar: dirty wood booths, cigarette burns scarring the plank, flickery TV blaring in one corner, half a dozen patrons who looked as though they'd taken root on their seats. And that was where he got into the discussion with the hollow-cheeked, half-drunk old man on the stool next to him.

He'd had just enough beer to bemoan his restricted freedom, without going into details. That was how it started. The old man squinted at him out of bloodshot thyroidal eyes, scratched at a bald pate speckled with liver spots, sucked at a straight shot of cheap well bourbon, wiped his mouth with the back of a gnarled hand, and made a noise like a chicken having its neck wrung.

"Freedom?" he said. "What you think that is, sonny, freedom?"

"Just another word for nothing left to lose."

"Huh?"

"Line from a Kristofferson song."

"Who the hell is Kristofferson? What's he know about freedom? Listen, you want to know about freedom, you ask somebody who does know. You ask me."

"All right, you tell me what it is."

"It *ain't*, that's what. Ain't no such thing. It don't friggin' exist. One of them magician's tricks . . . what you call 'em?"

"Illusions?"

"Yeah, illusions. Buy me a drink, I'll tell you why."

Cape bought him a drink.

"Everybody wants freedom," the old man said. "That's what they think they want. Go anywhere, do any damn thing they please any old time. Be their own boss. That about it?"

"More or less."

"More or less, my ass. That's it in a nutshell. But what they don't understand, not until they been around the horn a few times, not until they get to my age, is that life don't allow it. You hear me, sonny? Life don't ever allow freedom, so it don't exist except in people's minds."

"Why doesn't life allow it?" Cape asked him.

"Restraints, by Christ. Shackles. Chains. That's what life is—yours, mine, everybody's. Whole lot of big rusty links tying us up start to finish, first squall to your last. Don't matter where we go, what we do." The old man licked his lips with his mouth wide open; what teeth he had left were the color of tobacco in the dim light. "Buy me another drink, I'll give you some for-instances."

Cape bought him another drink.

"When I was a punk kid I joined the merchant marine," the old man said. "Salt in my blood, adventure in my eye. Gulf of Mexico, Caribbean, South China Sea, Pacific Ocean—I been up and down and across 'em all. Been through the Panama Canal more times'n I can count. You think I had your so-called freedom the whole time I was helping haul freight halfway around the friggin' world?"

"You tell me."

"Hell, no, I didn't. Wasn't no different than when I lived at home. People all the time telling me what to do, when to do it, how to do it. Captains, first mates, second mates, dock bosses, pissants and dumbfucks and niggers. Putting chains on me, every one of 'em."

Cape said, "You didn't have to keep wearing them."

"Is that a fact?"

"Could've thrown them off any time, couldn't you?"

"How? Jump ship in some banana port?"

"That's one way."

"I thought so, too, and that's what I did when I had all I could stand. Jumped ship in Venezuela, spent six months boozing and beachcombing, gettin' my ashes hauled and taking on odd jobs when the money run out. You think I had any of your freedom then?"

"You tell me."

"Hell, no, I didn't. Still had the chains put on. Bartenders, whores, cops, immigration assholes, people I did the odd jobs for. Do this, do that, don't do this, don't do that. Same thing when I finally come back stateside, same thing until I got too goddamn old to work ships or any other man's job—somebody always around to put on the chains. You want to know what the heaviest chain of all is, the one ties up a man the tightest? Buy me a drink, and I'll tell you."

Cape bought him another drink.

"Money," the old man said. "Green stuff, filthy lucre. Can't go nowhere, can't do nothing, without it. Got to have money, and that means you got to carry the chain. No getting rid of them heavy links no matter what you do."

"How about cutting all your ties, moving out into the wilderness, living off the land?"

"That don't save your ass. Chains out there, too. Nature's one—storms, floods, blizzards, wildfires. Sickness. Accidents. Not enough food, nobody to talk to. Don't think loneliness ain't a chain, sonny, because it is."

"I know it," Cape said.

"Damn straight. Women, there's another big one. You married?"

"Not anymore."

"Quit her or she quit you?"

"I quit her."

"Good for you," the old man said. "I had three wives, quit all three. And two live-in girlfriends and more one-night stands than you could shake a dick at. Couldn't wait to get rid of one so I could go whoring after another. What you think I called it when I shed a woman?"

"Getting your freedom back."

"That's it. Only soon as I got rid of one set of female shackles, there I was all wrapped up in another. Linked to this or that one for nearly fifty years, and for what? Ten times more whining and complaining than fucking, that's what for. I look back on it now, I figure I'd've been better off if I hadn't laid a single one of 'em. Just yanked my shank, pulled my pud, jerked my joint instead."

"No freedom in that, either, I suppose."

Strangling chicken noise. "Hell, no. Just a hairy palm and a sore pecker."

"You live alone now?" Cape asked.

"Wish I did. Chains there, too, but not as heavy as the ones my son puts on me. Live with him and his bitch of a wife. She hates my guts, don't want me in her house—house, she says, it's only a friggin' trailer. Calls me a dirty, drunken old man to my face. Which is what I am, and proud of it, but I don't want to hear it from her. Davey, that's my son, he was an accident, only accident I ever had and not my fault, but he took pity on me and brought me up here from San Pedro a couple of years ago. I liked it better in Pedro, chains weren't so heavy down there, like I said, but I couldn't afford to live alone no more. Drank up all my Social Security money. So here I am in Tahoe, drinkin' on a goddamn allowance. Allowance! Like when I was a snot-nose kid. Last place I'll ever be, settin' on this stool most days and nights until my liver gives out and Davey and his trailer trash can plant me for good."

"Sad story," Cape said sardonically. "Loaded with pathos."

"You think so? Well, you're wrong. I had my life, and it wasn't so bad, neither, chains and all. I'd do it all over again, except maybe for the women. No, hell, the women too. I ain't really no pud-puller. No, I'm not complaining, sonny. Not like you. You're the one feelin' sorry for himself."

"Me? The hell with that."

"What else you been doing since we started gabbing? Cryin' about how you been boxed in, can't leave Tahoe, can't get your freedom back. If that ain't feelin' sorry for yourself, I dunno what is."

"You don't know me, old man."

"Don't I? I seen a thousand like you in my time. Didn't I tell you I was the same myself once? Fighting the chains, chasing around after something nobody's gonna find because it don't exist."

"You don't know what I'm looking for, either."

"Freedom. Ain't that what you been pissing and moaning about?"

"More than that," Cape said. "A lot more than that."

"Such as what?"

"New places, new experiences."

"More chains."

"Life by the balls," Cape said, "with both hands."

"Hah! That's a good one, that is. Life by the balls with both hands. Life's gonna grab *you* by the balls with both hands, you don't watch out."

"Maybe it already has. Maybe that's why I want to grab back."

"There you go again, sonny. Pissing and moaning and feelin' sorry for yourself."

"I tell you I'm not. Not anymore."

"Sure sounds like it to me. What's eatin' on you, anyhow? More than just that freedom crap, ain't it?"

"No."

The old man showed his tobacco-colored teeth in a sudden grin. "Why, hell, I bet I know what it is. You ain't chasing so much as you're being chased. You're on the run."

"Wrong. Nobody's chasing me, old man."

"On the run, by God. How come? What you running from?"

Cape swallowed the last of his beer.

"Listen," the old man said slyly, "I can help you. I been on the run myself a time or two, I know a few tricks. Buy me another drink, I'll tell you what they are."

Cape shoved off his stool, picked up what was left of his change, and walked out of there.

Damn old man. Damn corrupt, wiseass, half-smart old reprobate.

He was wrong about freedom, and he was wrong about one other thing. The heaviest chains weren't made of money or the demands or expectations of others.

The heaviest chains were the ones you put on yourself.

23

Two voice-mail messages when he got back to the Grand, one logged in at 4:52, the other at 7:25. Both from the same man.

First one: "Cape, you know who this is. I'm in big trouble, I need to talk to you right away. Call me as soon as you get this. Don't talk to anybody else first." Followed by a local number and an extension.

Second one: "Cape, where the hell are you? Call me!"

Boone Judson.

Scared.

Cape replayed the messages twice. Judson's voice was ragged, with rips in it that let the fear leak through. He went into the bathroom, doused his face in cold water to get rid of the last of the beer muzziness. When he came out again, he called the number Judson had left. A woman's voice answered. "Cabins in the Pines. How may I help you?" He asked for number fourteen.

Buzz, buzz . . . and Boone's voice, shrill and shredded, said, "Hello? Cape, is that you?"

"It's me."

"Christ, about time. Where've you been?"

"Big trouble, you said. Name it."

"Not on the phone. You know what it is."

"What I don't know is where you fit in."

"Not on the damn phone."

"Why call me? What do you think I can do for you?"

"I can't go to the cops, I don't know anybody else I can take a chance on. Tanya's gone. She . . . two days ago, only now—"

"Now what?"

"No. Forget it."

Cape said, "She came to see me on her way out of town."

"She what?"

"I found her waiting in my room. How'd she know where to find me, Boone? How'd you know?"

"What'd she want from you? Money?"

"Answer the questions."

"How many times do I have to say it? Not on the phone!"

Cape said, "The sixteen thousand—that's what she was after."

Hissy breath. "You give her any of it?"

"I don't have it anymore."

"None of it?"

"Not a dime."

"Cape, listen—I've got to get away from here. I should've gone with Tanya, should've listened to her. . . . A thousand? Haven't you got at least that much you can let me have?"

"What do I get in return?"

"What do you want?"

"A full explanation. Who gave you those photographs, why you and Tanya came to Tahoe, the whole story."

"Bring the thousand, and I'll lay it out for you. Right away, Cape. Soon as you can get here."

"Cabins in the Pines. A motel?"

"South Lake Tahoe, not far from where you are."

"What's the address?"

Boone rattled it off. "No cops, Cape," he said then. "Bring the law, and I'll make them believe you were in on it, I swear I will."

"No cops."

"You don't come alone, I'll know it before you get to me."

Cape said, "Just stay put," and broke the connection.

Cabins in the Pines was off Pioneer Trail, up on the hillside one intersection beyond Black Bart Road. Tanya must have been heading back there on Friday. Spotted him following her, turned too soon so she could lose him. Either that, or she'd made a mistake—unfamiliar territory, preoccupied, scared—and had to drive around herself until she found the right street.

Cape rolled by the motel entrance, twice. Almost nine-thirty, full dark, night-lights and moonshine giving him a clear scan of the property. It was set in thick woods, one gravel road leading in and uphill; a handful of close-in cabins built of shaggy-bark logs were visible from the street in front, the ones higher up hidden in dense stands of pine. Quiet, and private: trees and distance separated the cabins from one another.

He drove back downhill, along Pioneer Trail to the next intersection, then a short way up the street that paralleled the one the motel was on. He parked the 'Vette there, walked back around the block to Cabins in the Pines, walked in past the lighted office as if he belonged there. Nobody came out to challenge him.

He followed the road, keeping to shadow along its edge. Short gravel arms branched off to two-car parking spots for each cabin, the arms marked by signposts with numbers burned into the wood and spotlights angled upward from the ground so you could read them. The first signposts he passed were 1 and 2, which made 14 one of the higher-ups.

When he neared cabins 11 and 12, he could see the road's terminus, a circle like the bulb at the end of a thermometer. Two vehicles were parked there, a distance apart from each other—one large, one small. Spotlit paths led off at angles from the circle into the trees. Diffused light filtered through thickly knit branches on the 14 side, but he couldn't make out the cabin itself. The one on the opposite side, 13, was completely dark.

Cape moved deeper into the woods' shadow, eased his way up to the nearest of the parked cars. Now that night had fallen, the temperature had dropped several degrees, and a cool wind off the lake made swishing, rattling noises in the trees; the wind and the pine needles underfoot muffled any sounds he made. Bent low, he ran to the rear of the smaller car.

Pale blue Mitsubishi. Hertz sticker on the rear bumper.

Still in a crouch, he crossed to the other vehicle. SUV—a Chevy Suburban, not new, white paint pitted and streaked with dirt. Personalized California plate: RTLDSCP. He eased along the driver's side, tried the door. Locked. He went back around to the passenger side. Locked.

From there he went up into the woods. The pines grew close together, and the spaces between them were clogged with ground cover and dead limbs. Slow going. Noisemaking, too; he waited until the wind gusted before taking each step. The path to number 14 was thirty yards or so to his left. The ground spots set at intervals along it cast enough light so that he was able to maintain a parallel course.

It took several minutes to reach a point where he could make out the cabin. A light burned over the door, a softer glow outlining the curtained window adjacent. When he was abreast of the cabin, he crept to within twenty yards and stopped in the shadow of a split-boled pine. From there he had a mostly unobstructed view of a narrow porch, the cabin door.

He thought again of Tanya's little automatic, the one he'd dumped in San Francisco. Schizoid feeling: wished he still had it, was glad he didn't. He'd never fired a gun in his life. Try to use one in circumstances like these, he was liable to do himself more harm than good.

He buried his hands in his empty pockets, leaned back against the pine to wait.

Five minutes ticked away, by the faint luminous dial of his watch. Ten. Nothing changed at the cabin. The only sounds were out here where he was: wind, night birds, rustlings in the undergrowth, a car coming partway up the road to one of the lower cabins.

Fifteen minutes.

Twenty.

Cold and the leaning position built a cramp in one leg. Cape flexed and massaged it away.

Twenty-five.

Thirty.

And the door opened—was yanked open—and a man came out onto the porch.

Boone Judson's size and squat shape, but not Judson. The nightlight over the door shed enough illumination for Cape to distinguish his features. Younger, darker, beetle-browed, thinning black hair. A stranger—yet familiar. And not because of the super-ficial resemblance to Judson.

Rollo. Who else?

He stood irresolute for a few seconds, staring down the path toward the parking circle. Turned then, slammed his hand hard against the door behind him. Went back into the cabin, leaving the door open so that Cape had an oblique view inside that told him nothing. A few seconds later Rollo reappeared, thumped down off the porch onto the path.

Cape hesitated. The impulse to go after Rollo, brace him, was strong; but in the darkness, with all the twigs and dry needles underfoot, he'd be heard long before he got close. Sure as hell Rollo was armed. That was the whole point of this trap, wasn't it?

He stayed put, watching Rollo hurry out of sight. After a minute or so he heard the cough and throb of an engine starting. Gears meshed, tires churned on gravel.

Another minute, waiting and watching the open cabin door. Nobody else showed there. Cape made his way out of the woods, as quietly as he could. Crept up the steps and eased his head around for a look through the open doorway.

One big room, pair of queen-size beds on one side, sitting area and kitchenette on the other. And Boone Judson lying facedown across the nearest bed, arms outflung, knees touching the floor. Black-scorched wound in the back of his head, above the hairline. Blood spattered over his pink scalp, what was left of his dust-colored hair; blood on the exposed sheets under his head. Shot once point-blank, execution style, not long after Cape's phone call.

Judas goat, scapegoat. Centerpiece of a frame.

Cape stayed where he was. Quick scan of the room. Only one thing caught his eye, a ring of keys on the table in the kitchenette. He moved then, sideways to the table. Car keys, Hertz tag on the ring. He swept them up, backed away to the door and outside.

He was sweating; the wind dried it, left it on his skin like a sheen of ice as he hurried down the spotlit path. At the circle he approached the Mitsubishi. First key he tried wouldn't unlock the driver's door; second one did. He opened it with the tail of his jacket wrapped around his hand. The dome light revealed empty seats, empty floor.

He shouldered the door shut, went around to the rear. The

same key unlocked the trunk. He raised the lid, using the key to do it, not touching the car itself.

"Jesus!"

Death-smell. It made him gag, recoil. The pale trunk light showed him the blanket-wrapped mound stuffed in there; and where one of the folds had pulled loose, the black-mottled face, protruding tongue, one staring eye.

Tanya.

Strangled.

Long time dead, Thursday-afternoon dead.

Cape slammed the trunk lid shut with his forearm. He pulled the key out, used his jacket lining to wipe it clean before throwing the ring down. In his mouth was a sick, brassy taste—the taste of fear. Worse than he'd expected, much worse. Trap, frame—blood-bath. And no easy way out, maybe no way out at all. Stupid to let Rollo walk away, stupid to think he could just turn him in to D'Anzello and then walk away himself—

Sudden light show. Swirls, pulses of red and blue at the motel entrance below.

Police cars. Two, three, four swinging in off the street. No sirens, just their roof flashers creating crazy colored patterns against the backdrop of trees and darkness.

Sure, sure, sure. The first thing Rollo had done was to put in an anonymous call to the local law.

Cape plunged headlong into the woods.

24

NIGHTMARE run: grotesque shapes, hidden obstacles that tripped and hindered him, dry branches poking, clutching like fleshless finger bones. There was no pursuit as far as he could tell—they hadn't seen him, they were busy back there at the cabin. But he couldn't make himself slow down.

He lost all track of time; the woods seemed to go on and on, endlessly. When he finally broke through the perimeter, it took him seconds to realize he was on the street where he'd parked the Corvette. Through a haze of sticky wetness he located it thirty yards downhill. He stumbled along uneven pavement to the 'Vette, leaned hard against cold metal as he fumbled the key into the door lock. Breath rattled in his throat; he couldn't seem to drag in enough oxygen.

Headlights sliced around the corner from Pioneer Trail below.

Cape threw himself inside, slammed the door, flattened across the passenger bucket. The beams swept uphill toward him, whitening the interior. Swept past without slowing.

He lay there until the pain in his chest eased and he could breathe more or less normally. His hands shook when he sat up. He had to steady one with the other to insert the key into the ignition.

Better once he got the car moving. The shakiness subsided. But the sticky wet kept oozing out—thick, oily, sour.

He made a U-turn, drove down to Pioneer Trail, turned left away from Cabins in the Pines. After a quarter of a mile a stoplight marked a major intersection. He turned there, toward the lake. Pretty soon Lake Tahoe Boulevard appeared ahead. Bright lights, traffic, people . . . the law.

The Corvette was another trap.

Distinctive, conspicuous. And D'Anzello had the plate number. How much time before every cop in California and Nevada had it on a hot sheet? An hour, two hours? Maybe not even that long. . . .

But he had to stay mobile; on foot his chances were zero. He was no car thief—it was the 'Vette or nothing. Just keep driving, keep moving. Stay off the major streets and roads. Use the backstreets.

And go where?

No place to run, no place to hide.

The wetness kept running down from his forehead. More than just sweat—a salt taste at the corner of his mouth. Blood. From a deep gash in the skin over one eyebrow; probing fingers brought awareness of stinging pain. Of other hurts, too, on his face and neck and hands. All torn up from his flight through the woods.

Have to do something about that right away. Blood made him even more vulnerable, more conspicuous.

Service station ahead, not crowded, not too well lighted on the side where the restrooms were. He pulled in there, parked in as much shadow as he could find. First-aid kit in the glove box. He took it to the door marked *Men*.

Inside, he locked the door and looked at himself in the cloudy mirror. Scratches, scrapes, the one gash; his face a streaky mess of sweat, dirt, blood. He washed in cold water, covered the gash with antiseptic and a bandage. His clothing wasn't too bad—a couple of tears in the shirt, another in the jacket. He used paper towels to clean off smudges of dirt, a crimson splotch, clinging twigs and pine needles.

Better. Not so much like an accident victim.

Back into the rolling trap.

Side streets, hunting now for a bar with dark, off-street parking. Found one: the Buckhorn Tavern. The name was familiar— one of the places he'd been in earlier. Dark inside, handful of customers and a bartender who minded their own business. Cape ordered a double shot of Jack Daniel's, tossed it off. Its heat steadied him. He ordered another shot, single this time. The last thing he could afford to do was muddy up his thinking with too much liquor.

He asked about a public phone. The bartender pointed him to an areaway that led to the restrooms. Phone but no directory. Most taverns had a bar copy, so he went back there and asked. The bartender said maybe they had one, maybe they didn't, he didn't have time to go hunting. Cape slapped down two singles, his change from the drinks. That bought him a cheapjack grin and the immediate appearance of a dog-eared local directory.

He moved over to where the light was better, flipped the book open to the yellow pages. Scanned through the listings under Gardeners.

Small boxed ad on the second page: R. T. Landscaping Service. RTLDSCP. R. T. Landscaping Service. R. for Rollo?

No individual's name in the ad, no address—just a phone number, and the words "Complete Lawn Care and Garden Maintenance. Residential/Commercial."

Cape leaned his forehead against the wall. No place to run, no place to hide, no place else to go. Think. Think!

Short, dark, pudgy like Boone Judson. R. T. Landscaping Service . . . residential/commercial. Lakepoint Country Club. Lakepoint, Lakepoint . . . something else about the country club . . .

My son Gary . . . he works part-time as a caddy. . . . Lilith works there, too, in their payroll department . . .

Justine.

Justine what? What was her last name?

Breakfast buffet waitress Friday morning, saying the name in a stiff voice, saying—

Blank.

Saying—

Come on, Cape, think! Saying—

"Will there be anything else, Ms. . . . Ms. . . . "

President's name. Dead president's name—

Coolidge.

He tore into the directory again, this time to the white pages, the C's.

J. Coolidge, 2294 Lakeview, S. Lake Tahoe.

25

H E didn't have far to drive, just a mile or so back toward State-line and then across Lake Tahoe Boulevard, but it seemed to take a long time to get there. Every car, every set of head-lights, was a potential threat. So far, his luck was holding; none of them belonged to the law.

Lakeview Drive curled along a short section of shoreline in the middle of town, private homes and a few motels on the lakefront side, small apartment complexes and a scatter of houses on the in-shore side. Two-two-nine-four was one of the complexes, a dozen units in two facing rows on one level; a lighted sign in front said Rest Haven Apartments. Cape parked in tree shadow down the block, returned on foot.

Behind the sign was a bank of mailboxes, each one labeled with the tenant's name. J. Coolidge was number 5. That unit was toward the rear, and when he got there he found the front window curtained and no light leaking out at the edges.

He went up onto a tiny railed porch, thumbed the bell. Empty echoes inside. He thumbed it again, hard and long, in his frustra-tion. Nothing, nobody home.

Justine wouldn't still be working at the Grand, not this late. Out

somewhere for the evening. Wait around until she came home?
What else could he do?

Cape came down off the porch. And then stopped, swinging
his head around, when he heard the crunch of approaching steps
on the path.

Kid, fifteen or sixteen, wiry build, dark brown hair in a buzz
cut. The path lights were bright enough to limn his features as he
neared: high cheekbones, distinctive almond-shaped eyes.

The kid slowed to a wary standstill a few feet away. "Hi. You
looking for somebody?"

"Gary? Gary Coolidge?"

"That's me. Who're you?"

"My name's Matt. I'm a friend of your mother's. No, that's not
right. An acquaintance of your mother's. We met at the Lakeside
Grand the other day. She didn't mention me?"

"Uh-uh. She invite you over?"

"No, she didn't."

"So how come you're here?"

"To ask her for a favor. An important favor."

"Yeah?" Suspicion in the almond-shaped eyes. "You look kind
of messed up. Like you were in a fight or something."

"Not a fight. Running around in the woods where I should'nt've
been," Cape said. "When's your mother due home?"

"Before midnight, she said. She and Lilith went to dinner and
a flick. You know who Lilith is?"

"Yes." Midnight. Long, long time.

Gary said, "Mom tell you about me, too?"

"She talks a lot about you. Proud of you."

"Well, I'm proud of her, too. We watch out for each other."

"That's the way it should be."

"What's this favor you want from her?"

"Her or Lilith. Or you."

"Me?"

"She told me you caddy at the Lakepoint Country Club. So you
know some of the other employees."

"Some."

"A landscape gardener named Rollo?"

"Rollo? Nah."

"You sure?"

"None of the gardeners is named Rollo, I'm sure of that."

"R. T. Landscaping Service," Cape said.

Blank look.

"Short, pudgy, dark-skinned man. Brown eyes, thinning black hair. Drives a white Chevy Suburban with a personalized license plate—RTLDSCP. Uses drugs."

"Oh, man . . . Stickface. That asshole."

"Stickface?"

"That's what we call him. If he ever smiled, his face'd crack in two. He tried to sell me some speed once. Right there at the club."

"What's his real name?"

"Torres, Targes, something like that."

"Think, Gary. I need to know for sure."

He thought. And shook his head. "I don't remember."

"First name, if it isn't Rollo?"

"If I ever heard it, I forgot it. We just call him Stickface."

"Any idea where he lives?"

"No. How'd I know?" Suspicion showed again in the kid's expression. "How come you're so interested in this guy? If it's drugs—"

"It's not."

"I hate that stuff, man. I don't want anybody uses drugs messing around my mom."

"I swear to you, my needing to find him has nothing to do with drugs. It's personal, and it's urgent."

"How come urgent?"

"Because I'm in a bad spot, and he can get me out of it," Cape said. "Would you recognize his name if you saw it written down?"

"I dunno, maybe."

"I'll give you fifty dollars if you check the phone book for me."

"Fifty! No sh—no kidding?"

"In cash."

The kid said, still wary, "You can't come in with me. You'll have to wait out here."

"No problem. Just make it fast, okay?" Cape fished a twenty and a ten out of his wallet, pressed them into Gary's hand. "The other twenty when you come back."

"Even if I don't have his name?"

"Yes. But I really need it, name and address both."

"Well, I'll try." Gary gestured toward a public area—lawn, benches, a tiny playground for kids—that stretched between the two rows of apartments. "You can wait over there."

The kid was gone more than twenty minutes. Cape, sitting tensed on one of the benches, had begun to sweat and fidget by then. When he saw Gary appear from inside the lighted unit, he was up and over there in a hurry.

"No listing in the phone book, Matt. But I got his name another way." Grinning, pleased with himself.

"Good man."

"Lilith's computer," Gary said. "She works at home sometimes, she's got all her Lakepoint files stored here. And I know her access code. She wouldn't like it if she knew I tapped in, but for fifty bucks . . ."

"What's his name?"

"Tarles, T-a-r-l-e-s. Some first name—Rolando."

Rolando Tarles, Rollo for short. "Address?"

"Four-sixty-five Columbine Road."

"South Lake Tahoe?"

"Yeah. I don't know where Columbine Road is."

"I've got a map in the car." Cape handed over another twenty, added an extra ten. "Thanks, Gary. You may have just saved my ass."

"What'd Stickface do to you, anyway?"

"Helped steal something from me that I'm going to get back, one way or another."

"Money?"

"More important."

"What's more important than money?"

"Something that damn well does exist," Cape said. "Freedom."

26

Columbine Road.

Short residential street, lower-middle-class neighborhood like the one off Black Bart Road. Number 465 was the last house in the block, butted up against the fenced perimeter of a cemetery. Shake roof, redwood siding, at least fifty years old. Screened-in front porch and plenty of shrubs, flowers in neat rows—advertisement for R. T. Landscaping Service. Driveway on the fenced side, pickup truck pulled in close to a detached garage.

All of it was dark, not even a night-light showing. And no sign of the Chevy Suburban anywhere in the vicinity.

Cape said, "Shit," between clamped teeth. He made a U-turn, cut off Columbine on the nearest cross street, and went looking for a place to abandon the Corvette. Took him fifteen minutes to find one: grammar school, teacher's parking lot behind an ungated chain-link fence, pocket of darkness under a big acacia tree. Safe enough there until morning. By then it wouldn't matter one way or another if it was spotted.

He found his way back to Columbine Road. Three sets of headlight beams picked him out of the dark; he walked through them and past them without hesitation, the way a resident would. None of the cars was official. Nobody hassled or paid attention to him. A middle-aged guy walking his dog even said hello as they passed each other.

Rollo's house was still dark, deserted. A porch light was on at the house next door, but the windows there were all black rectangles. Lights burned in the houses across the street; a woman moved behind an undraped picture window in the last one as Cape passed, but she neither glanced out nor paused. A TV set in there was tuned loud enough for the sound of canned laughter to reach all the way to the street. The woman's attention was on the screen.

Cape climbed the steps to Rollo's screened porch. There was a bell; he didn't touch it. The screen door was locked, so the one behind it to the house would be, too. He backed down the steps. The undraped window across the street showed him the TV blaring away, to an empty room now. He moved quickly to the driveway, followed it back to where the pickup sat. Black lettering on the driver's door read R. T. LANDSCAPING SERVICE. He tried the handle. Locked.

The backyard was another, smaller advertisement, cemetery-fenced on one side, tree-fenced on the other two. Dark, private. He checked the rear door to the house. Secure in the jamb, probably by a deadbolt. The window next to it was also secure; so were the windows set into the far side wall.

In the backyard again, Cape ran his fingers along the edges of the window adjacent to the door. Single pane, not thick, the putty holding it old and cracked. One sharp blow ought to break it.

Take the risk?

Better than waiting out here in the cold. Christ knew when Rollo would decide to come home.

Cape took off his jacket, wrapped it around his right arm. When the wind made some noise, he drove his elbow against the glass.

It broke cleanly, the crash loud enough in his ears to freeze him in place. A dog began to bark somewhere, not close by. He strained to hear other sounds. Rasp of his breathing, thud of his heart, the wind. He kept on waiting, listening. The dog's barking grew sporadic, finally quit altogether. Another minute. Two, three.

Nothing.

He moved then, picked jagged shards out of the bottom frame

so he wouldn't slice himself up when he reached inside. The catch was jammed or rusted in its groove. Took him another two or three minutes to wiggle it loose, and still more time to slide the sash upward far enough for his body to fit through. He was sweating again, shivering from the cold, when he hoisted himself over the sill. A glass sliver dug into the heel of his hand as he swung down; he barely felt it.

Utility porch. He bumped into a smooth, hard surface that his fingers told him was a washing machine. He groped his way along the washer and a dryer next to it, found a wall, shouldered along it until he reached a doorway. Then he was in the kitchen. Enough moonlight dusted through a window in there to show him the shapes of a sink, refrigerator, dinette table and chairs.

At the sink he began opening drawers that extended below on both sides. The fourth one yielded a flashlight. He shielded the lens with his hand before he switched it on. The batteries were good, the beam steady.

Cape crossed the kitchen, letting just enough light spill out between his fingers to guide him through a swing door into a small dining area. Adjoining that was the living room. His nostrils dilated as soon as he started in there.

Marijuana—the thick, acrid reek of it.

He went all the way in, playing snatches of light. Ashtray on a coffee table overflowing with roach butts. Two dirty highball glasses, a mostly empty fifth of Jim Beam, plates littered with food remnants. Sleeper couch pulled out and made up with rumpled sheets, blankets, for a recent overnight guest—Boone Judson, probably. Rollo keeping the scapegoat fed, watered, and stoned before the slaughter.

The living room had nothing else to tell him. The remainder of the house was two small bedrooms, one outfitted as an office, and a messy bathroom. In Rollo's bedroom, the nightstand drawer held a well-used crack pipe and other drug paraphernalia. Heavy user, all right—high when he murdered Vanowen, no doubt stoned the afternoon he strangled Tanya and tonight at Cabins in the Pines. Much easier to kill another human being when you had chemical assistance.

Cape checked quickly through the closet, the dresser drawers. Nothing. The office contained a beat-up rolltop desk, a Radio

Shack computer and printer, a metal file cabinet. Desk first, then
the cabinet.

Know your enemy.

Evidence. More than enough for him, if not for Captain D'Anzello.

Release papers from Arizona State Prison in Yuma, dated six
years ago. Four years served of a four-year sentence for unspecified
crimes.

Bill of sale, three years old, for a secondhand fourteen-foot
boat and an Evinrude outboard motor.

Receipts from Baxman Marine, Pine Beach, for boat storage.

Thirteen thousand dollars in cash, a gold Rolex watch that belonged to J. T. Sturgess, and Vince Mahannah's unique turquoise-
and-silver ring.

Cape sat in a butt-sprung armchair in the living room, a fireplace
poker close beside him.

Working it out and waiting for Rollo.

Midnight.

The silence was so acute it had the effect of pulsing sound in
his ears, like surf in a shell. He'd been tight-strung for a long time.
Now a kind of lethargy was creeping through him.

Twelve-thirty.

Emotions growing dull, thoughts sluggish. The aches in his
body bone-deep, as if burrowing. His eyelids had a weighted feel.

One-fifteen . . .

Sudden noise.

Cape heaved up out of the chair, groggy with sleep, still caught
in shredded fragments of the dream. For a few seconds Anna was
still there with him, screaming accusations, and he could hear
echoes of Mary Lynn's voice saying, "If you don't beg God's forgiveness, you'll burn in the fires of hell," his old man down in
Florida laughing drunkenly and saying in the raspy voice of the

other old man tonight, "Life's gonna grab *you* by the balls, you don't watch out." Then all at once voices and fragments were gone, replaced by a jarring awareness of where he was—the room, the darkness, the marijuana stink.

And the noise again. No, noises, outside on the street.

Car engine, percussive music.

He rubbed grit from his eyes; shapes swam into focus. The front window was only a few steps away. He staggered to it, parted the curtains just enough so he could see the street.

Kids, not Rollo. A Trans Am with its radio playing loud rap, drawn up in front of the house opposite, engine throbbing, headlights reaching all the way to the cemetery fence. Couple inside in a heavy clinch. The door to the house over there opened suddenly, and a man in striped pajamas came charging out, yelling.

Cape quit watching. He made his way back to the chair but didn't sit. His head ached fiercely, his heart still hammered. The luminous dial of his watch gave him the time: 2:57. He'd been asleep more than an hour.

The Trans Am's engine growled, its tires squealed. Seconds later those noises and the beat of the music died away. Silence came down thick again.

Three A.M., and still no Rollo.

Not home by now, he wasn't coming. Spending the night somewhere else.

Cape switched on the flashlight, not bothering to shield the beam now, and followed it into the kitchen. He splashed his face with cold water from the sink tap, drank thirstily from cupped hands. The bitter taste in his mouth remained.

Weakness in his limbs, lower back pain, the fierce headache—rough shape all around. But it was only fatigue, stiffness from sleeping propped up in the armchair, the constant tension. He'd be all right. Just get moving. Bad-luck Cape, but still sound enough for a lot more miles if he could just get free and back on the open road again.

First things first. He remembered keys in one of Rollo's desk drawers. Spare key to the pickup in the driveway?

27

THE Ford truck was a piece of crap. It took Cape nine or ten tries, the exhaust farting gouts of smoke, before the engine caught and held; and when it was running, it had a catch in it like an asthmatic's wheeze and a tendency to misfire if you bore down too hard on the accelerator. The gearbox and clutch assembly were as cranky as the engine: the one ground, the other slipped and strained every time he shifted.

Small price. The heater worked the way it was supposed to, at least, and the gas gauge showed an almost full tank. Along with the early-morning darkness, the pickup's warm shell provided protective coloration. Proof of that when a police car passed him as he approached Stateline on mostly empty Lake Tahoe Boulevard. Neither of the cops inside even glanced at him or the R. T. LANDSCAPING SERVICE painted on the door.

Cave Rock.
Nobody home.

Pine Beach.
Long, tense drive back through South Lake Tahoe, north on

Highway 89 through a precipitous stretch high above Emerald Bay that left him even more fatigued. Tiny hamlet strung along a deep curving inlet strewn with anchored pleasure craft. A pair of marine retailers and repair outfits, one at each end of the inlet; the second was Baxman Marine.

Small place just off the highway: fenced-in boatyard, tiers of dry-docked boats, corrugated iron building not much larger than a house, long T dock with slips. And on the gravel strip in front of the fence gates, a bulky shape that the Ford's headlights identified as a light-colored SUV. Cape slowed to a crawl as he passed by. Chevy Suburban, slewed in at an angle so that the rear license plate was easy to read: RTLDSCP.

He kept going for another hundred yards, swung over onto the verge in front of a darkened grocery store. This late, the highway was deserted. It stayed that way as he made his way back to Baxman Marine.

The only lights visible anywhere inside the fence were nightlights, some on poles along the dock that made the lake water gleam blackly, like an oil slick. Among the shapes and shadows, nothing moved that he could make out. He turned to the Suburban. The driver's door wasn't locked; he pulled it open long enough to determine that the interior was empty. At the front, he laid a hand on the hood—cold, the metal spotted with dew. Parked here for quite a while.

The two halves of the yard gate were joined but not secured, a padlock hanging loose through one of the chain links. Cape slipped inside, picked his way past the dry-docked boats and a scattering of trailers and other equipment. On the near side of the corrugated building was a set of wide double doors; a regular-size door was cut into the near end wall. He tried that one first. Locked. An ear laid against the cold metal picked up faint wind-generated vibrations, no other sounds. He stepped away from the downspill from the nightlight above, went to check the double doors. Also secure.

This place must belong to somebody Rollo knew well enough to entrust him with keys. He paid a cut-rate price for storage, too. Was that why he'd come here tonight, to take his boat out on another night run somewhere?

Cape went down to the slips, out onto the dock. Halfway along he found a fourteen-foot skiff, its engine tilted up out of the water and tarp-covered. He lifted a corner of the tarp; the outboard was an Evinrude. The other boats moored here were a mixed lot, no two alike. Odds against more than one fourteen-footer outfitted with an Evinrude. Odds on that this one was Rollo's.

So where the hell was he?

As Cape pivoted, started back, his attention caught and held on the rear of the warehouse building. He stopped again, looking up there.

Lighted window in that wall, the glow framing it steady, bright. The window was high up, too high to see through without a ladder. The light might be an office nightlight, but there wasn't much sense leaving one on inside with the grounds lit up the way they were.

He slid a hand into his jacket pocket, brought out the ring of Rollo's spare keys. Then he hurried up and around to the single door in the front wall. The third key he tried fit the lock, turned the bolt. He held a breath, edged the door open and himself through, shut it fast behind him.

The light at the rear came from a desk lamp in what appeared to be an office walled off by dirty glass and particleboard. From this distance Cape could make out little of what was inside. The outpouring of lamplight extended only a few yards; most of the warehouse space was heavily shadowed, its concrete floor crammed with shapes large and small, identifiable and unknown. No sounds came from the office or anywhere else. The hush had a crackling quality that raised the hairs on Cape's scalp.

Ahead was an aisleway that seemed more or less clear. He moved that way, one slow step at a time, a hand extended to fan the air in front of him. Stacks of board lumber, plywood sheets, wooden forms, a boat skeleton on a davit. Lathes, drill presses, table saws. Smells, distinctive in the cool air: sawdust, paint, linseed oil, turpentine. And something else, as he drew nearer the office—faint, unpleasant, not quite distinguishable yet.

Twenty yards away, he sidestepped a hand truck that appeared suddenly in front of him—and ran into another object. It cracked glancingly off his forehead, rattled and swayed sideways, then swung back at him in the darkness. He ducked, crouched, as metallic echoes rolled through the interior. The thing kept on swaying above him—some kind of caged droplight suspended from a ceiling beam.

No one appeared inside the office, no other lights came on.

The echoes died away. The faint swishes made by the droplight died away. Dead hush again.

Cape straightened slowly. When his pulse rate dropped, he moved forward again. The lamp in the office must be a nightlight after all. Rollo wasn't there, wasn't anywhere on the premises. . . .

Wrong again, Cape.

Rollo was there, all right. He'd been there all along.

Cape saw him as soon as he reached the partly open door. Dirt streaks in the glass wall gave the office a wavy, surreal look, as if he were seeing it through a sheen of murky water. Desk, swivel chair behind it, and Rollo in the chair, sprawled backward, head hanging to one side, mouth open and eyes squeezed shut, the expression on his face one of agony.

Cape pushed the door all the way open, went in by one pace. The unpleasant smell was strong here, ammoniac. He breathed through his mouth as he moved nearer the swivel chair.

Up close, Rollo wasn't much to look at—broad through the chest, thick-lipped, potbellied. The front of his khaki pants was urine stained. No blood visible on him, no marks of violence—but the left sleeve of his soiled white shirt was rolled up, a piece of rubber tubing tied tightly around the bare upper arm. Cape stepped closer. On the floor between the desk and chair, the broken remains of a hypodermic syringe glinted in the lamplight. Scatter of grainy white powder down there, too.

Overdose. Self-administered.

Dead?

No. Breath hissed and rattled faintly in Rollo's throat; the pulse in his wrist was a weak flutter. In a bad way. Coma, maybe. He'd die if he didn't get medical treatment soon.

Cape hesitated, scanning the office. The bottom drawer in the desk had been pulled out; inside, its lid thrown open, was a metal lockbox partly filled with plastic baggies. Grainy white powder, rock crystals, loose marijuana, rolled joints. Drug deli. The owner of Baxman Marine had a profitable sideline; Rollo was an associate, his best customer, or both.

There was a phone on the desk. Cape lifted the receiver with a piece of paper, tapped out 911. Five terse sentences, the last one giving Rolando Tarles's name and the address of Baxman Marine.

The dispatcher asked him to repeat, asked for his name; he broke the connection.

He was still boxed in, almost as tightly as before. If Rollo died, he could still lose his freedom for good. D'Anzello could claim he'd administered the overdose. No proof that he hadn't. No proof that he wasn't Rollo's partner in the robbery, that he'd had nothing to do with the deaths of Tanya and Judson.

One chance left. Just one.

He beat it out of there, fast.

28

RUBICON Bay.

As before, the gate to the Vanowen property stood open. Cape accelerated through and down, not trying to be quiet about his arrival. The house was lightless until he rattled to a stop in front and swung out; then one came on inside. Stacy Vanowen's BMW was the only car drawn in under the carport.

The shaded porch bulb sprayed whiteness over Cape, but the door stayed shut. He leaned on the bell. It was another thirty or forty seconds before the door finally opened. Stacy Vanowen peered out at him, wide-eyed. She wore a robe and slippers, but her haggard expression, the smokelike marks under her eyes, her twitchy movements, said he hadn't woken her up.

"My God," she said, "what're *you* doing here?"

"I have to talk to you."

Side-to-side head movement, as though she were trying to throw off confusion. "It's almost five A.M. Whose truck is that out there? Where's your car?"

"Inside. Please."

"You look . . . Have you been in a fight?"

"Not the kind you mean."

He moved forward, crowding her slightly. She gave ground, her eyes showing bewilderment and more than a little fear.

"I don't understand what you're doing here," she said.

"You will. Where can we talk?"

". . . The living room."

She led him into a darkened room, put on an overhead light. Cape had an impression of space, blue-and-brown color scheme, native stone, beams, paintings, objets d'art. None of it registered clearly. The hammering in his temples was acute now; pain radiated along his spinal column, up the back of his skull, and his vision had lost clarity.

Stacy Vanowen said, "You'd better sit down. You look ready to collapse."

"Feel like it."

"Do you . . . want a drink? Brandy?"

"Brandy, yes." He sank down on soft cushions, leaned his body forward instead of settling back. Too comfortable, and he might not be able to remain alert. "You'd better have one yourself."

"Not at this hour."

"You'll need it when you hear what I have to say."

For a few seconds she watched him, chewing on her lower lip. Then she went away; came back pretty soon with a well-filled snifter in each hand. Cape drank half of his. It was like swallowing fire. He watched her sit down a distance away from him, knees together, tucking the folds of the robe around them, clutching her snifter tight between both palms as if they were cold and she was using it to warm them.

"Now what's this all about?" she said. "What happened to you tonight?"

"Same thing that's been happening to me ever since I came to Tahoe. Tied up in chains, put into a box."

"Chains, box . . . you're not making sense."

"I know who killed your husband," Cape said.

Blink. Blink.

"Who, why, how, the whole thing. You won't want to believe it, but it's true."

"Why won't I want to believe it?"

"Too close to home."

"You're still not making sense. The man in the ski mask . . . you know who he is?"

"A landscape gardener, ex-con, and drug dealer named Rolando

Tarles. Rollo for short. That's his pickup outside. He pulled the trigger, but your sister did the cocking and aiming."

Bug-eyed stare. "Lacy? You . . . that's . . . why would she—"

"Money and hate. In that order."

"What money? You can't mean Andrew's. She's not in his will—"

"No, but you are. Property, bank accounts, stock portfolio—you get it all, don't you?"

"Lacy and I aren't close, you know that."

"You still let her come around whenever she feels like it, dole out pocket money, presents. She's smart, manipulative. Play her cards right, patch things up with you, and she'd wind up with plenty for herself. Big gamble, big payoff."

Stacy Vanowen sat rigidly. Her face had a milky cast, more alabaster than marble, the veins beginning to show. Abruptly she brought the snifter to her mouth, spilling some of the brandy, and drained it in one convulsive swallow.

She said, "What reason would Lacy have to hate Andrew?"

"He had everything she didn't, for one. She called him an arrogant bastard, a prick, a control freak, a serial fornicator. Said he made a pass at her once at a party."

"That . . . doesn't surprise me. I knew he had other women, not all of them strangers to me. Lacy may have hated him—I hated him myself sometimes—but enough to plan his death? No."

"She hates all men," Cape said. "The kind of hate that breeds destruction. Blame it on your father, what he did to her when she was a child."

Stacy Vanowen winced, said nothing.

"She's ruthless when it comes to men. Uses and abuses them whenever she can—she as much as admitted that to me. She used Rolando Tarles. She used Boone Judson. She used me."

Silence.

"The whole thing was a setup, start to finish," Cape said. "Rollo works at Lakepoint Country Club, she plays golf there—I saw the two of them talking there the other day. She found out he'd been in an Arizona prison. Seduced him probably, gave him a chunk of cash, promised him a bigger payoff later—wrapped him up so tight he'd do anything for her."

Headshake. Denial or reflex, Cape couldn't tell which. She was no longer looking at him.

"Rollo brought Boone Judson into it," he said. "Prison connection—they were both in Yuma at the same time. The plan was to let Judson believe it was a gambling scam, his bread and butter, with you and your husband and Vince Mahannah as the marks. That's one reason he was picked. The other was his size and build, same as Rollo's. Lacy got her hands on the photos of Vanowen and Mahannah; Rollo took the ones of you. He sent them to Judson as the convincer, used some excuse to make sure Judson kept them in his possession. The photos and his body type made him the perfect fall guy for your husband's murder.

"So far, so good. But then things began to go wrong. Judson had picked up a partner, Tanya, he didn't tell Rollo about. He figured he'd need seed money for the gambling scam here, so he and Tanya worked another one in San Francisco first. He made the mistake of inviting me into the Frisco game. And another by bringing Tanya with him to Tahoe."

Cape's mouth was dry. He drank off the rest of the brandy, swirling it through his mouth, before he went on.

"Tanya complicated Lacy's plans. She didn't fit into the frame as it was originally conceived. Then Tanya began to smell a rat. She wanted out, only she had no money of her own. Rollo must've let it slip that I was here—that's what brought her to my room at the Grand. When she couldn't get any money out of me, she went back to the motel where they'd been staying. My guess is Rollo was there alone, waiting for her—by then he'd already moved Judson to his own house for safekeeping. She was so desperate she tried to shake him down. He strangled her instead."

Stacy's head jerked up. "He . . . what?"

"Strangled her. Hid her body in the trunk of their rental car—later that day, after dark. I found it there tonight."

"Oh, God."

"But that didn't change Lacy's plans," Cape said, "any more than my showing up with the photos had at first. She figured to lay Tanya's murder off on Judson. And mine. She used sex to find out how much I knew, decided it was a little too much, and told Rollo to kill me, too, during the fake robbery.

"When I talked to her yesterday, I said some things that convinced her I was even closer to the truth. And she said something that should've told me then that she was involved, only I didn't realize it until tonight."

"What did she say?"

"'It's not every night you see a man get his face shot off.' She claimed she didn't know what had happened at the poker game until she heard the news on the radio. Sheriff's department wouldn't have given out that kind of explicit information, and the media wouldn't use it if they had. 'Brutally murdered,' yes. 'Face shot off,' no."

"That's not . . ." The rest of the words caught in her throat; she coughed them loose. "That doesn't prove Lacy did all you say she did."

"What happened tonight does. She still wanted me dead. So she tried to include me in the frame against Judson, make it look like we were partners and had a falling-out and killed each other. Right after I talked to her, she and Rollo set up a trap at the motel. But it was clumsy and obvious, and I didn't walk into it. If I had, I'd be dead now. Even so, I made the mistake of letting Rollo get away, and he boxed me in with the law. I've been running around all night, trying to find him or Lacy to get myself out of the box."

"Did you?"

"Get myself out? Not yet."

"Find Lacy. Or this man Rollo."

"Rollo, yes. Baxman Marine, in Pine Beach."

"I don't . . . Why would he go there?"

"He keeps a boat there. And the owner has a sideline—dealing drugs. Rollo may have been in on it with him. He was strung out after killing Judson, went to Pine Beach to get some of whatever he was using, and gave himself an accidental overdose."

". . . You mean he's dead?"

"Not yet. Barely alive."

"Will he die?"

"Maybe yes, maybe no," Cape said. "If he doesn't, the law ought to be able to get a confession out of him. Even if he does die, there's enough evidence to implicate him."

"What kind of evidence?"

"Money and items from the robbery, among other things. At his house. Nothing there that points directly at Lacy, but I'm banking that there's hard evidence against her somewhere. She's improvised and screwed up too damn much."

"I don't understand why you came to me," Stacy Vanowen said. "Why didn't you just go to the authorities?"

"None of the evidence against Rollo exonerates me," Cape said. "I don't want to give myself up cold if I can avoid it. I need help, some kind of leverage, and you're the only person I can turn to."

"How can I help you?"

"Have you got a tape recorder?"

"Tape recorder?"

"Is there one in the house? Voice activated, preferably."

"Yes. Andrew had one."

"Call your sister, ask her to come over here. I'll confront her, try to get her to admit something incriminating in front of you and on tape." Giving voice to the notion made it seem desperate, a little wild. The way he felt right now. "If that doesn't work, you could go with me when I turn myself in, tell Captain D'Anzello you believe me."

She bit her lip, still not making eye contact.

Cape said, "You do believe me?"

"I don't know what to believe."

"You know your sister, what kind of person she is. You know she's capable of everything I've said."

"Yes, I know what she's capable of."

"Will you help me?"

"I don't . . . I can't seem to think clearly. Another brandy . . ."

She stood, walked slowly across the room. Cape resisted an impulse to lean back and close his eyes; rubbed grit out of them instead. Tension, exhaustion . . . his thoughts had fuzz on them now. Better get up, move around, breathe some fresh air. The warmth in here was making him logy—

Car coming.

The sound, filtered but distinct, brought him alert. He started up out of the chair.

"Stay where you are. Don't move."

Cape swung his head. Stacy Vanowen was walking back toward him with a short-barreled revolver in her hand.

He stared at her, at the gun. She must've had it in the pocket of her robe all along. Another goddamn gun pointing at him.

"What's the idea? Who's that outside."

"Shut up. Damn you . . . just shut up."

The car noise stopped. A few seconds later the front door

opened, letting the wind thrum in briefly before it banged shut again. Quick footsteps.

Lacy.

She came into the room, swung her gaze from her sister to Cape and back again. She said, "You'd better let me have that," and plucked the revolver from Stacy's fingers.

"What took you so long? I couldn't've stood listening to him much longer."

"I was almost home when you called. You did fine, honey. Just fine."

Stupid Cape.

Snake-eyes Cape.

The two of them were in it together.

29

Now that Lacy had the gun, her eyes remained fixed on him, flat, cold, unblinking, like a bird's or a reptile's. Stacy Vanowen's marble look was nothing more than a thin veneer; her sister was the hard one—hard all the way through, except for a core of dirty ice.

Stacy leaned against the back of a couch, wobbly now, pale. Cape had already ceased to exist for her; all her attention was on the older woman. She said, "He knows everything."

Cape said bitterly, "I do now. Some act the two of you put on yesterday. Some act you put on just now. I fell for it both times."

He might just as well have been talking to himself. Lacy said, "It doesn't matter what he knows. Did he tell anyone else?"

"He says he didn't."

"Then we're all right. How'd he get hold of Rollo's truck?"

"I don't know. But he found Rollo somehow."

"Where?"

"Pine Beach. The place where he keeps his boat."

"The one damn place I didn't think to look. Where is he now?"

"In the hospital," Cape said, "in police custody."

Stacy said, "No, he's dead. . . . He *has* to be dead."

"Dead? How?"

"Drug overdose."

"Well, well. Good. Saves me the trouble."

"Lacy, please . . ."

"He wasn't dead when I left him," Cape said. "He'll talk when he goes into withdrawal. He'll sell out both of you."

"Shut up, salesman." Acknowledging him for the first time. Stacy said, "What if he isn't dead? What if he does talk?"

"Let him. Stupid drugged-out ex-convict—who'd believe him over the two of us? Take it easy, don't worry so much."

"I can't help it, I'm scared."

"I'll take care of you. Haven't I always?"

Cape said, "Sure you have. You've taken her right out of all this luxury and put her into a women's prison for the rest of her life."

"I said shut up."

"Or else you'll shoot me? You're planning to do that anyway. Question is, have you got the nerve to do it face-to-face?"

"You think I don't?"

"It's one thing to send somebody like Rollo out to do your killing for you, another to do it yourself."

"That's right. But you won't be my first."

"No?"

"No. Remember what I told you about dear old Daddy, how he finally shot himself for his sins? Well, he didn't. I'm the one who blew his head off. While he was sleeping in front of the TV, the night he raped my six-year-old sister for the first and last time."

Stacy clapped both hands over her ears. "Don't! Please don't! You know I can't stand any talk about that."

"I know, honey. I'm sorry."

"You didn't get caught that time," Cape said, "so you think you'll keep right on getting away with murder. But you won't."

"Yes, I will. Only you won't be around to see it happen."

"Too many killings, Lacy. Too many dead people all at once. Vanowen, Judson, Tanya, maybe Rollo. And now me. The law isn't stupid. They're not going to buy it. Too many holes, too many leaky patch jobs."

"Lacy . . ."

"Don't listen to him, sis. He's full of shit."

"No, he's right . . . too many dead people. My God, it was only supposed to be Andrew, nobody else. But then you had to make it all so complicated. . . . Tarles and Judson and the poker game. We should've just done it with the boat, a simple accident, the way I wanted to in the beginning."

"Don't you start in on me now," Lacy said. "It was a good plan, and it would've worked, nobody else would've gotten hurt, if Judson hadn't brought that woman with him, Cape hadn't shown up with the photos, Rollo hadn't gone crazy on speed. None of that was my fault. What else could I do but make the best of things, keep you out of it as much as I could?"

Cape said, "Don't believe it, Stacy. Her ass was the only one she cared about. She was afraid you couldn't handle the pressure. She's still afraid you can't."

"That's enough from you." A vein pulsed in Lacy's forehead. "One more word, and I'll kill you right now."

"Not here!" Stacy cried. "Not in front of me!"

"All right, go in the bedroom. Wait for me in there."

"Not in the house, Lacy, *please.*"

"I'll make it look like he broke in, tried to attack us—"

"Not in the house! Outside somewhere, the boathouse, I don't care, just not in the house. I couldn't stand to live here anymore. . . ."

"Calm down. I won't do it here."

"Promise? Promise me."

"I promise. Go in the bedroom. Take a Valium, no more than one."

"A Valium. Yes. You won't be long?"

"I won't be long."

Wobble steps, hurrying, and Stacy was gone.

Cape said, "She's about as close to the edge as you can get. She'll tip over when the police start throwing questions at her."

"Not with me there to hold her up." The gun flicked. "Stand up, salesman. Walk out to the front door."

Cape got to his feet, slowly. But that was all he did.

"Go on. Move."

"No," he said.

"Move!"

"Fuck you, lady. For the last five minutes I've been listening to the two of you talk about killing me as if I were no more than a bug. I'm a human being, dammit. I've had all the abuse I'm going to take from you. You want to shoot me, do it right here, right now. Blood all over your sister's expensive carpet."

She bared her teeth at him.

"Go ahead," Cape said. "Only Stacy'll have hysterics when she hears the shot and sees my bloody corpse. She'll crack for sure then, Valium or no Valium. I'd lay a bundle you won't be able to put her back together again."

"You son of a bitch."

"You can't win this game, Lacy. You're in way over your head. Both of you lose, whether you kill me or not."

"We'll see who loses!"

Cape took a sliding step toward her, watching the gun.

Reflexive pressure on the trigger.

He lunged, twisting his body sideways, just as the gun bucked. Slice of pain along his left side, noise like a thunderclap, stink of cordite, and in the next second he was on her. He smacked her arm with his forearm, drove it up as she fired again, the revolver close enough to set up a ringing in one ear. Then he caught a grip on the hot metal with both hands, wrenched it loose, threw it aside.

Lacy fought him like a cat, all claws and hisses and spit. Scratched him, tried to bite him. He threw her off; she came back with an upthrust knee that just missed his crotch. He lashed out with the heel of his hand—a sideswipe blow that caught her on the temple above the hairline, staggered her off balance into an end table. Some kind of urn flew off, shattered on the floor; Lacy went down with it, her feet tangled in the table legs.

Melon-thumping sound: the back of her head colliding with the thick wooden base of the couch.

Her body stiffened, seemed to draw in on itself. Her eyes rolled up until nothing showed but white. She flopped over on her side, twitching.

"Oh God what did you do to her?"

Stacy, in a doorway across the room. One hand hovered in front of her mouth, the other pressed an ear—speak no evil, hear no evil. He saw her chest heave, her whole body shake as if she were about to go into convulsions.

Cape backed away, looking for the gun. Found it, picked it up.

Lacy tried to lift herself up. Made it to her knees, fell back down. And twitched and tried to lift up and fell back down. Again, and again, more weakly each time, little scrambled sounds coming out of her throat. Concussion. Disoriented, no longer a threat.

"You hurt her you hurt her you hurt her . . ."

Sounds from Stacy as empty and senseless as the ones her sister was making. She stayed where she was, as if she'd been seized by paralysis. The convulsive movements slowed. All at once she slid down the wall, bonelessly, almost liquidly, to puddle on the floor. She sat there with her eyes squeezed tightly shut. See no evil.

Little sister, weak sister.

Weak link in this set of chains.

But all he felt was numb. He sat on the edge of the couch to catch his breath, inspect the wound in his side. Bloody, stinging, but not much more than a gash.

Bad-luck Cape had some good luck left after all.

He went looking for a telephone to find out just how much.

30

D'ANZELLO said, "Cape, you're a damn fool."

"I won't argue with that."

"Six times over. You could be dead right now."

"I know it."

"Why'd you go after Lacy Hammond like that, with the gun in your face? You think she wouldn't fire?"

"I told you why," Cape said wearily. "I told the DA why. It's all there in my sworn statement."

"Tell me again."

"I'd had enough, that's why. It was either jump her or let her kill me."

"You could've waited until you were outside. Used the cover of darkness to make your play."

"Better odds if I could rattle her enough so she'd lose her cool. She really didn't want to do it inside the house."

"You were lucky. Beat the odds."

"Sometimes you do, sometimes you don't."

"Pretty offhand reaction," D'Anzello said.

"I'm not trying to be offhand or smartass, Captain. I'm tired . . . hell, exhausted. Are you going to let me leave here pretty soon?"

"I don't know yet. I could charge you with any number of

felonies, you know. Withholding evidence, breaking and entering, car theft, assault."

Cape said thinly, "Lock me up in a cage. Is that what I get for handing you three cold-blooded murderers?"

"I didn't say I would charge you. I said I could."

"I was being used. Boxed in. Everything I did was because of that."

"And you're a man who hates being boxed in."

"That's right. Look, you've got my statement and my apology. Stacy Vanowen confessed; it looks like Tarles is going to make it, and you'll get a confession out of him if he does. You don't need me anymore. It won't do anybody any good to take away my freedom."

"True enough," D'Anzello admitted. "The DA pretty much agrees. He's licking his chops over the two sisters; he's not interested in you. He left it to my discretion whether to charge you or not."

"Well?"

D'Anzello leaned back in his desk chair, tapped the edge of a pen against a front tooth. "You don't strike me as the hero type, Cape."

"Me? I'm not."

"Took a lot of guts to do what you did. Most men wouldn't've been able to rush into the muzzle of a gun like that, even to save themselves."

"Are we back there again?"

"Most men wouldn't have gone up against a purse snatcher with a knife, either, the way you did in New Orleans."

Cape sighed. "I didn't know he had a knife when I chased him."

"Police report says you had no weapon, that you disarmed the man bare-handed. Sounds pretty heroic to me."

"Reflex, that's all."

"Just being a good citizen."

"Trying to be."

"Good citizen, good Samaritan, hero—all wrapped up in one package."

"If you say so."

"But the Matthew Cape who lived in Rockford, Illinois, the one we ran the background check on, wasn't like that at all. Quiet salesman type, Mr. Average. What changed that Matthew Cape into this one?"

Silent shrug.

"Come on, now," D'Anzello said. "What made you quit your job, leave your wife, buy a Corvette, start gallivanting all over the country? What gave you the sudden horror of being boxed in? What changed Clark Kent into Superman?"

"Superman. Jesus."

"Answer the question."

"Midlife crisis," Cape said. "Everybody has one, they tell me."

"I don't buy it."

"All right, then. I needed a change. I'd had enough of the dull life, I craved some excitement."

"That doesn't explain going up against knives and guns. Mild-mannered salesmen don't grow a new set of balls overnight."

"Maybe I just got tired of all the injustice and suffering in the world, decided to do something about it in my own small way."

"Crap."

"Or maybe I'm atoning for past sins."

"Uh-huh. Storing up points in heaven."

"Something like that."

"I want a straight answer. What makes Cape run?"

"I'm not running."

"I think you are," D'Anzello said.

"Listen, Captain, I've got to have some sleep. Either charge me, or let me go. Get it over with."

"I'm not going to charge you. You can leave, but not until you come clean about yourself. And give me some kind of guarantee that you can be found to appear as a prosecution witness when the case goes to trial in three to six months."

"I can't do that."

"No? Why not?"

Cape took a breath, dribbled it out. Then, "Okay. Okay, you want to know why I quit my old life and took up the new one, I'll tell you. I did it for the same reason I went up against the knife and the gun, the same reason I have the horror of being boxed in, the same reason I won't be available to testify at the trial, the same reason I hope to God you let me out of here quick. Because I'm living on borrowed time, and what little I have left is running out fast."

"Borrowed time? What—"

"I'm dying," Cape said. "I'll be dead in less than a year, maybe as soon as four or five months."

Long silence. "From what?" D'Anzello asked in a different voice.

"Rare blood disease. One hundred percent fatal."

"Sweet Jesus."

"Specialists in Chicago passed sentence nine weeks ago. I'll give you their names if you want them."

"No, I believe you." D'Anzello leaned forward, tight-lacing his fingers on the desktop. "What, uh . . ."

"Symptoms? Headaches, back and joint pain, increasing fatigue—you really want the whole list?"

"No."

"I can function more or less normally until the last stages, they tell me. Then it's a hospital bed, painkillers, last rites." Cape bent a smile in half. "Maybe I won't get that far."

"Is that what's really behind the heroics? Looking for a way to get yourself killed quick?"

"Hell, no. I want as much time aboveground as I can get. But if it happens suddenly, I won't shy away from it."

D'Anzello said slowly, "What about your wife? Your family?"

"What about them? They don't know."

"You didn't tell any of them? People who care about you?"

"I made damn sure none of them found out. You're the only one besides the doctors who knows."

"Why not your family?"

"My wife, my sister and her family, my father, all have their own problems. They don't need mine to make their lives any worse than they are. You didn't talk to any of them personally, did you? Tell them where I am?"

D'Anzello shook his head. "You just walk out on your wife? Is that why she's divorcing you?"

"No," Cape said. "I set it up so she caught me screwing another woman in our bed."

". . . That's pretty damn cruel."

"Not the way I look at it. The marriage was over anyway, hanging together by a thread. If I'd told Anna about my condition, it would've made her life even more miserable. She'd have tried to hang on out of duty, right to the end. She's a nurse—she wouldn't walk out on a terminal patient."

"There must've been another way—"

"What way? Disappear? She'd have worried herself sick, blamed herself, tried to find me—put her life on hold. Same thing if I'd told her the truth and then walked away. I couldn't let her suffer like that. I loved her once. Part of me still does."

Penetrating stare, as if D'Anzello was trying to cut away skin and bone to see inside his head. "I can't figure you out, Cape."

"Look at it this way. One quick hurt, and you heal pretty fast. Long, slow hurt, and the wound stays open, maybe never really heals at all."

"All right. I see your point, even if I don't agree with it."

"Same goes with the rest of the way I'm handling my death sentence, right? You don't agree with the traveling, the lifestyle. Well, I'll tell you, I've packed more living into the past few weeks, found out more about myself and this world, than in all my previous thirty-five years. And I'm hungry for more of the same."

D'Anzello opened his mouth, shut it again.

"There're a lot of different ways of dying," Cape said. "But when you boil them down, they amount to only two."

"You think so?"

"I know so. Hard and easy. I'm doing it easy."

"Doesn't sound so easy to me. Not the past few days anyhow."

"Even those were better than moping around Rockford, waiting passively for the Big Dark." He bent another smile, pushed back his chair. "Can I leave now?"

"Go ahead."

Cape went to the door, turned, and came back a couple of paces. "Think about it, Captain," he said. "See what kind of answer you come up with."

"Answer to what?"

"If you knew you had only a few months to live, what would *you* do?"